D1827670

On the RAILS

The **train** may fall in love with a station, but it has to go and it goes!

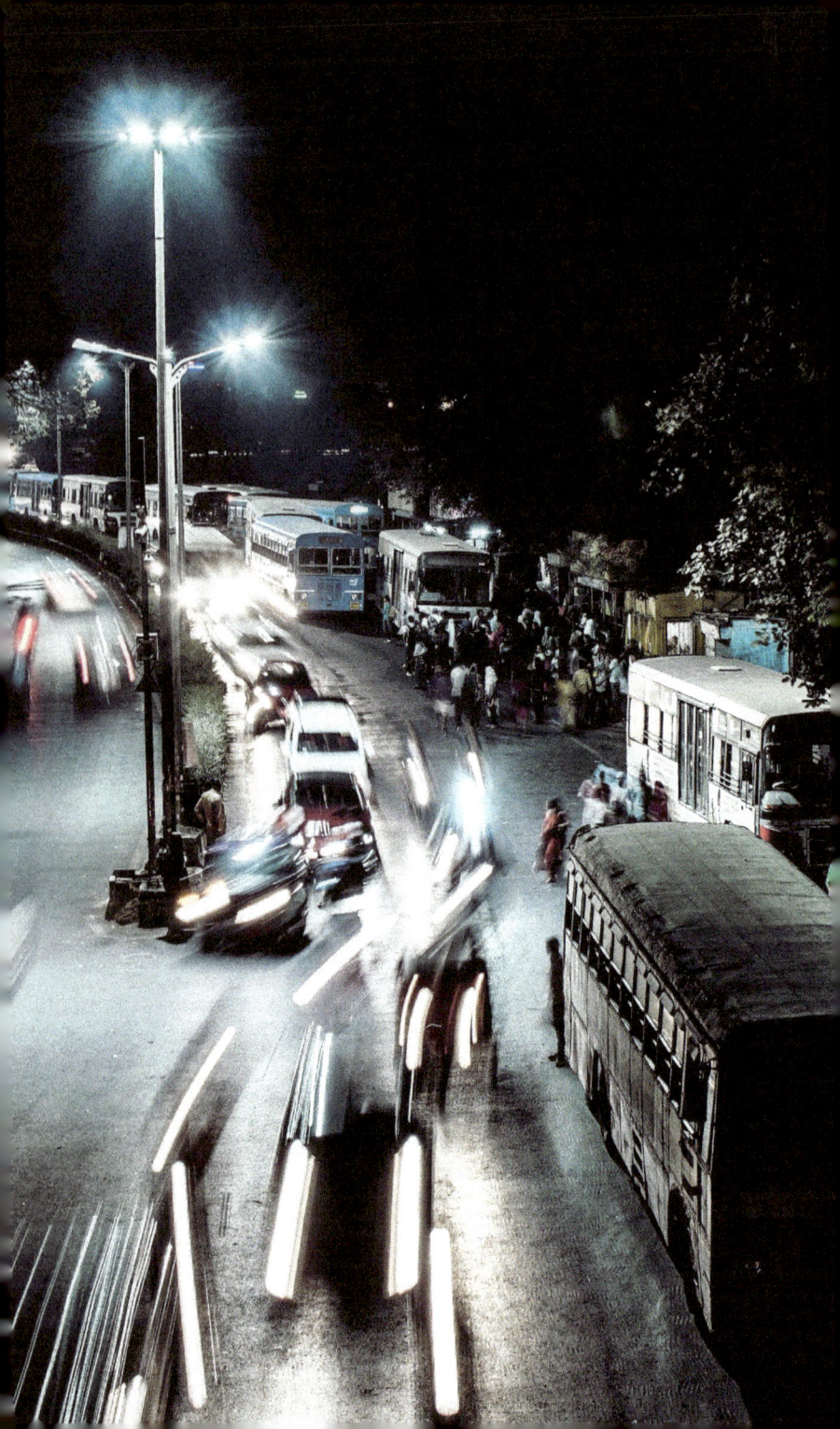

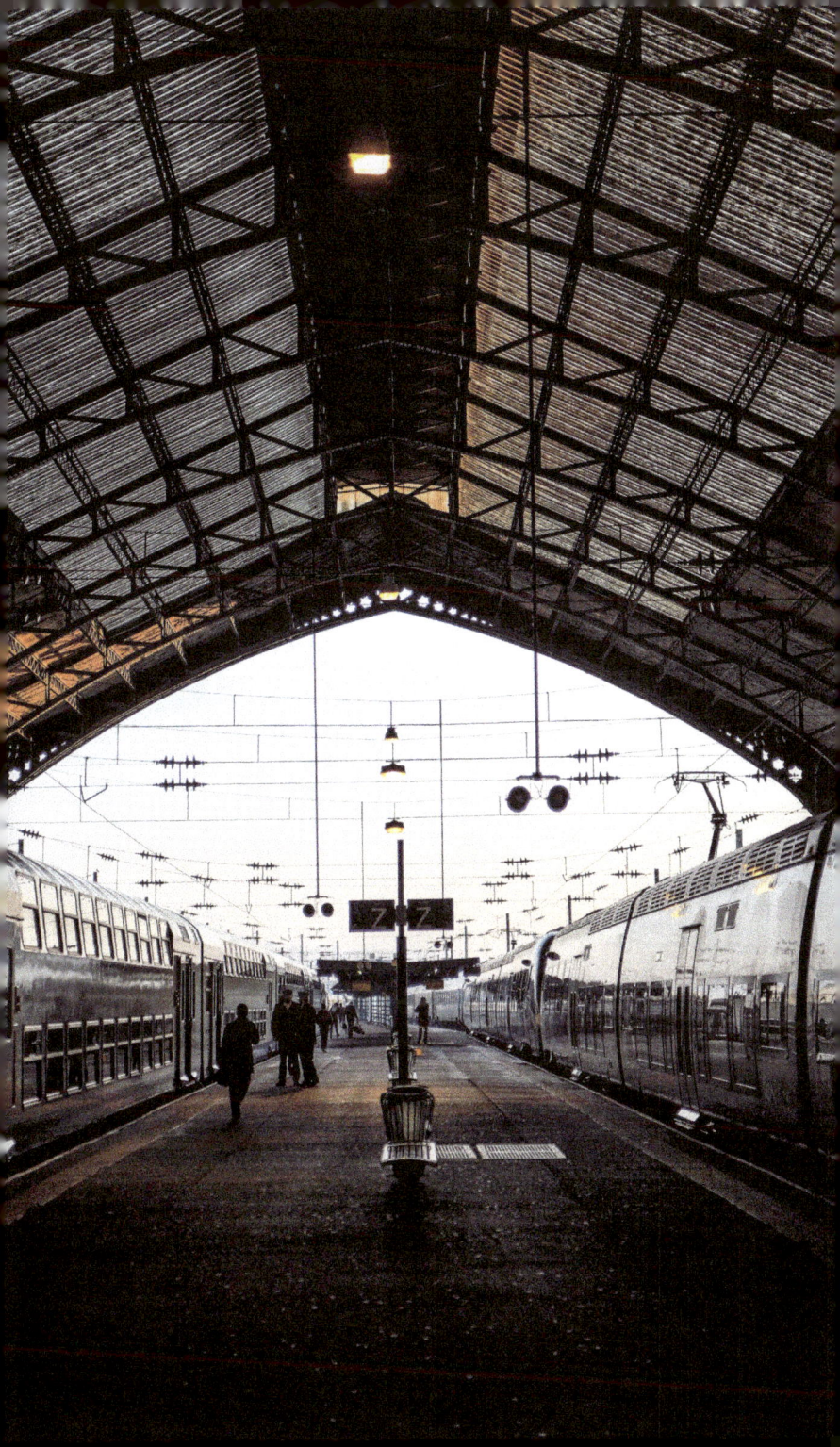

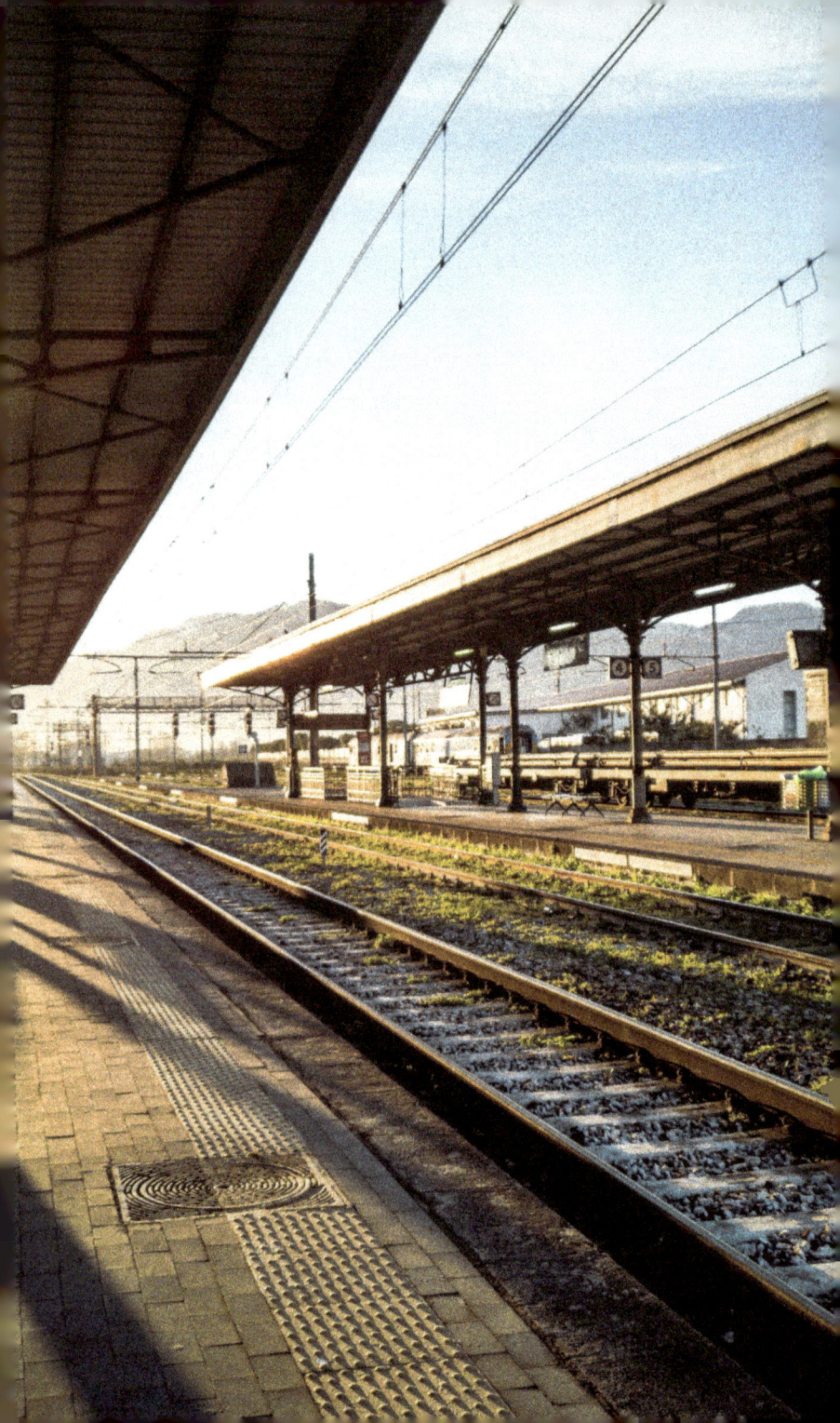

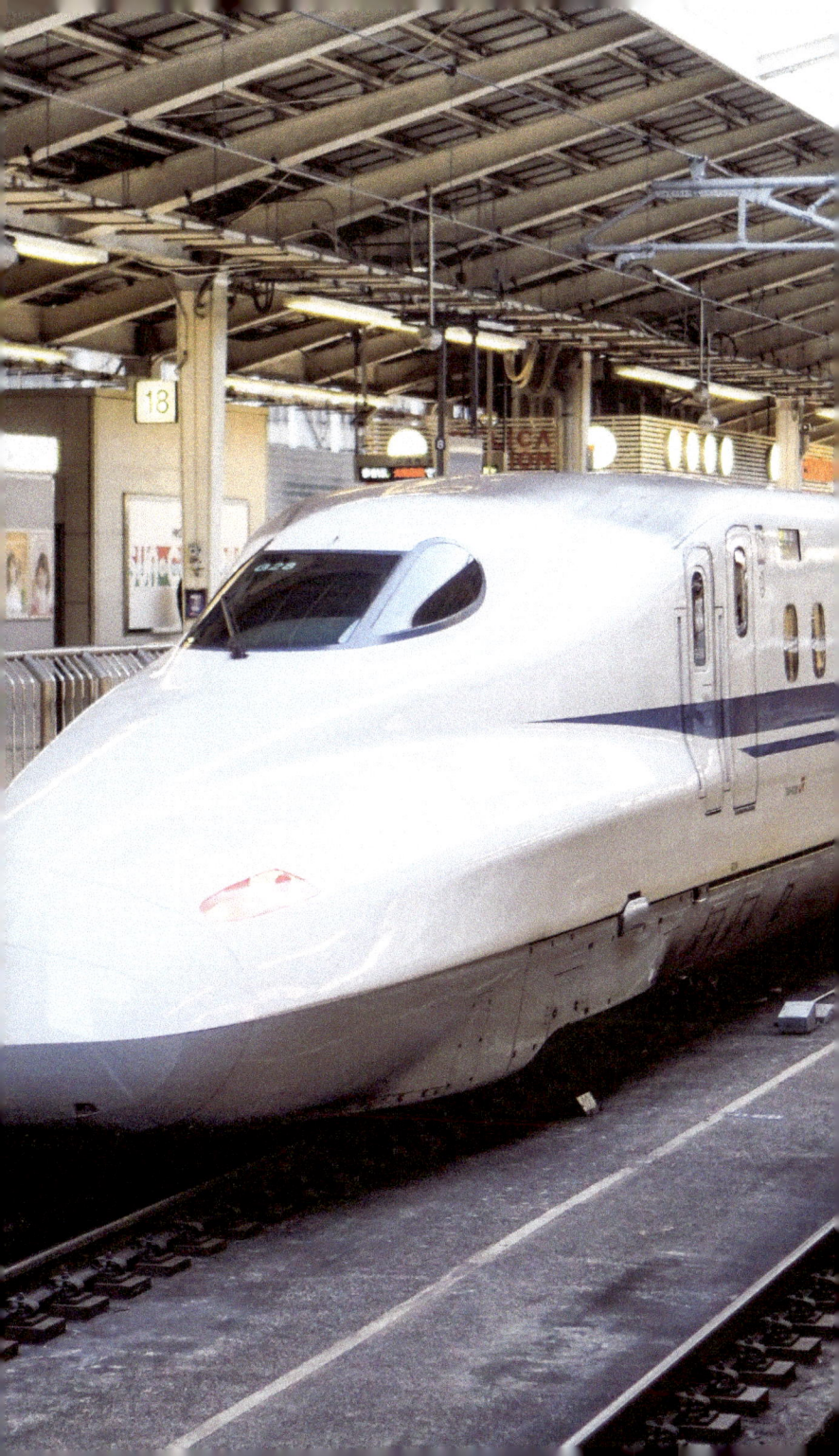

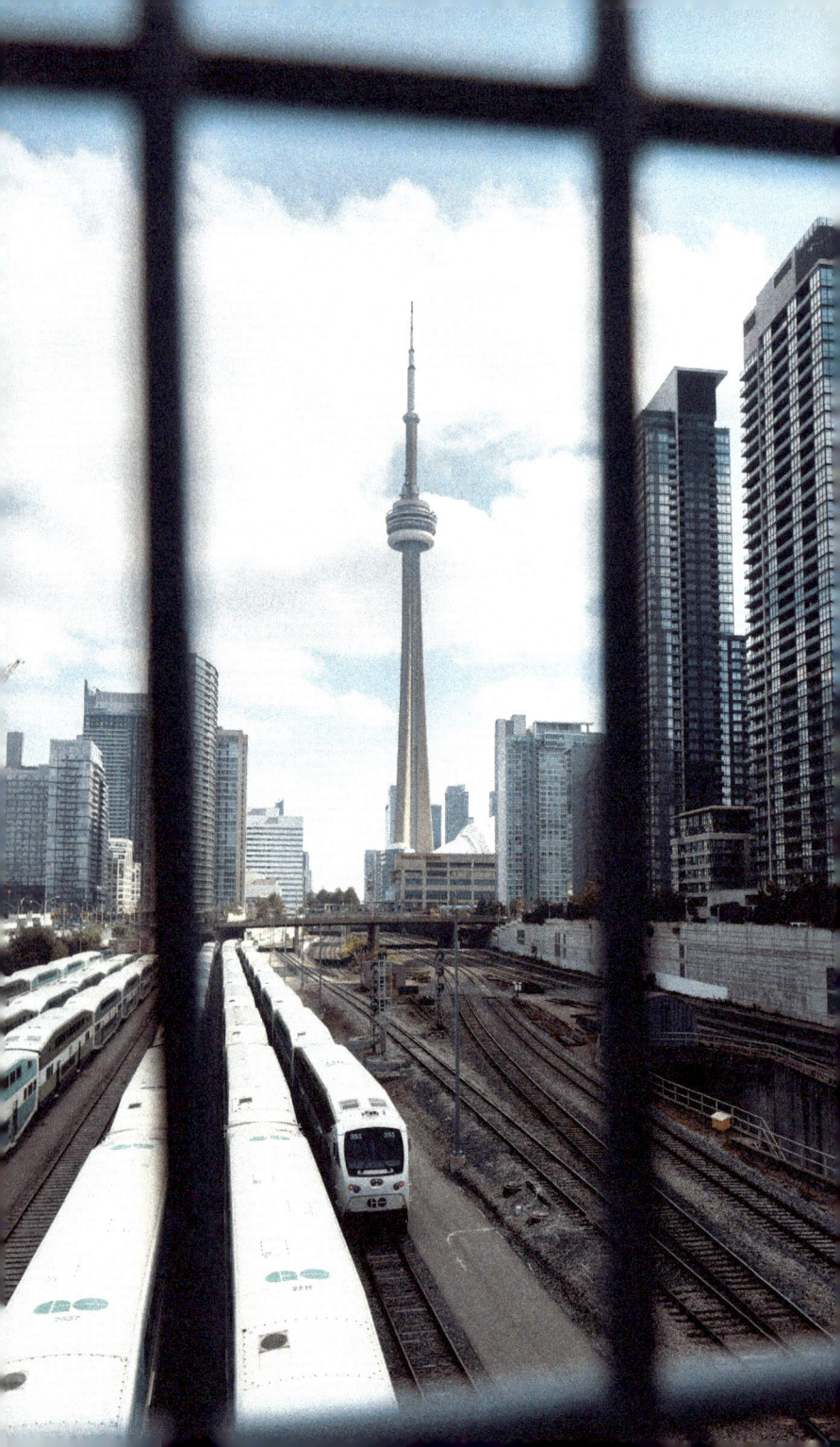

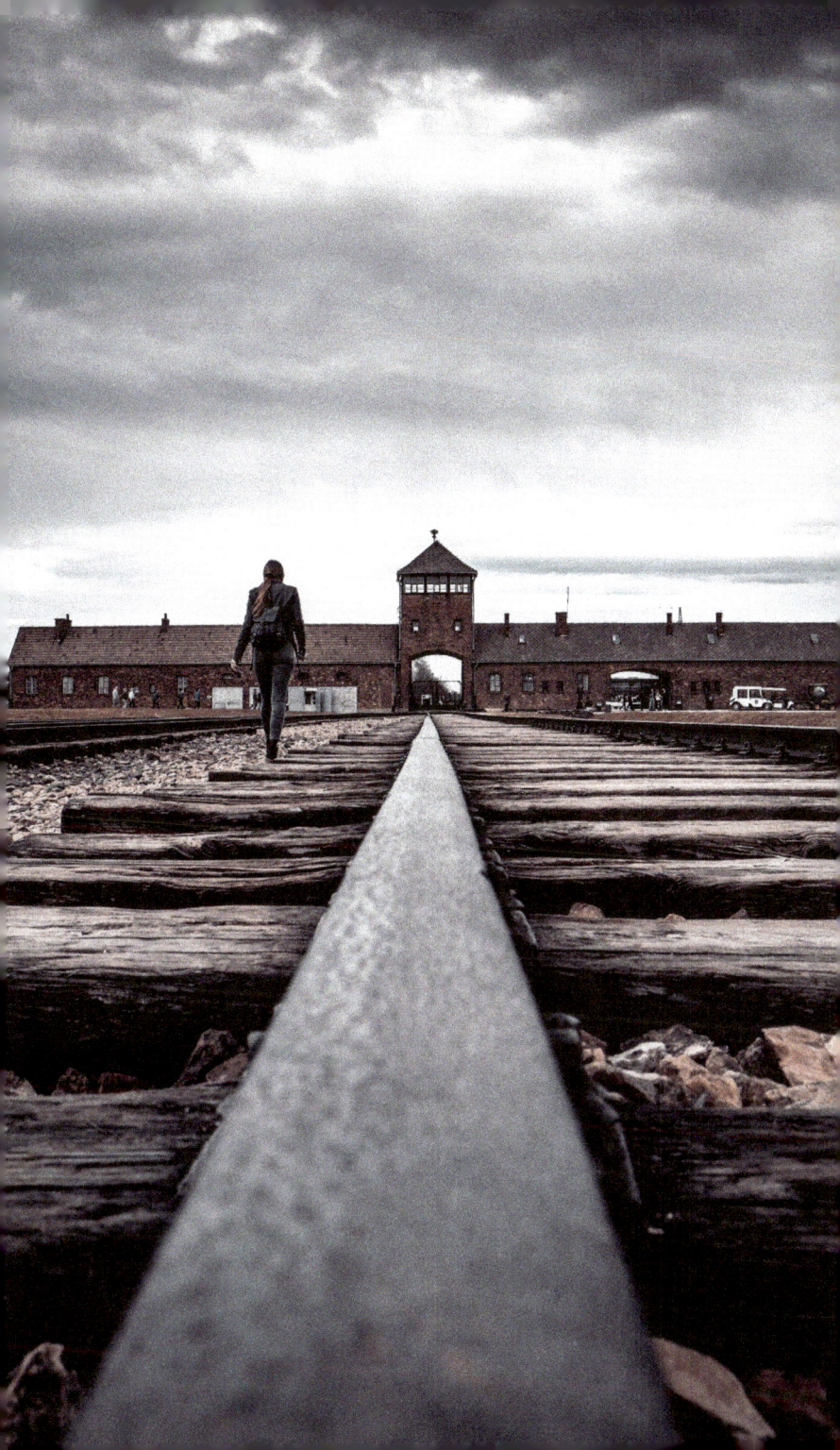

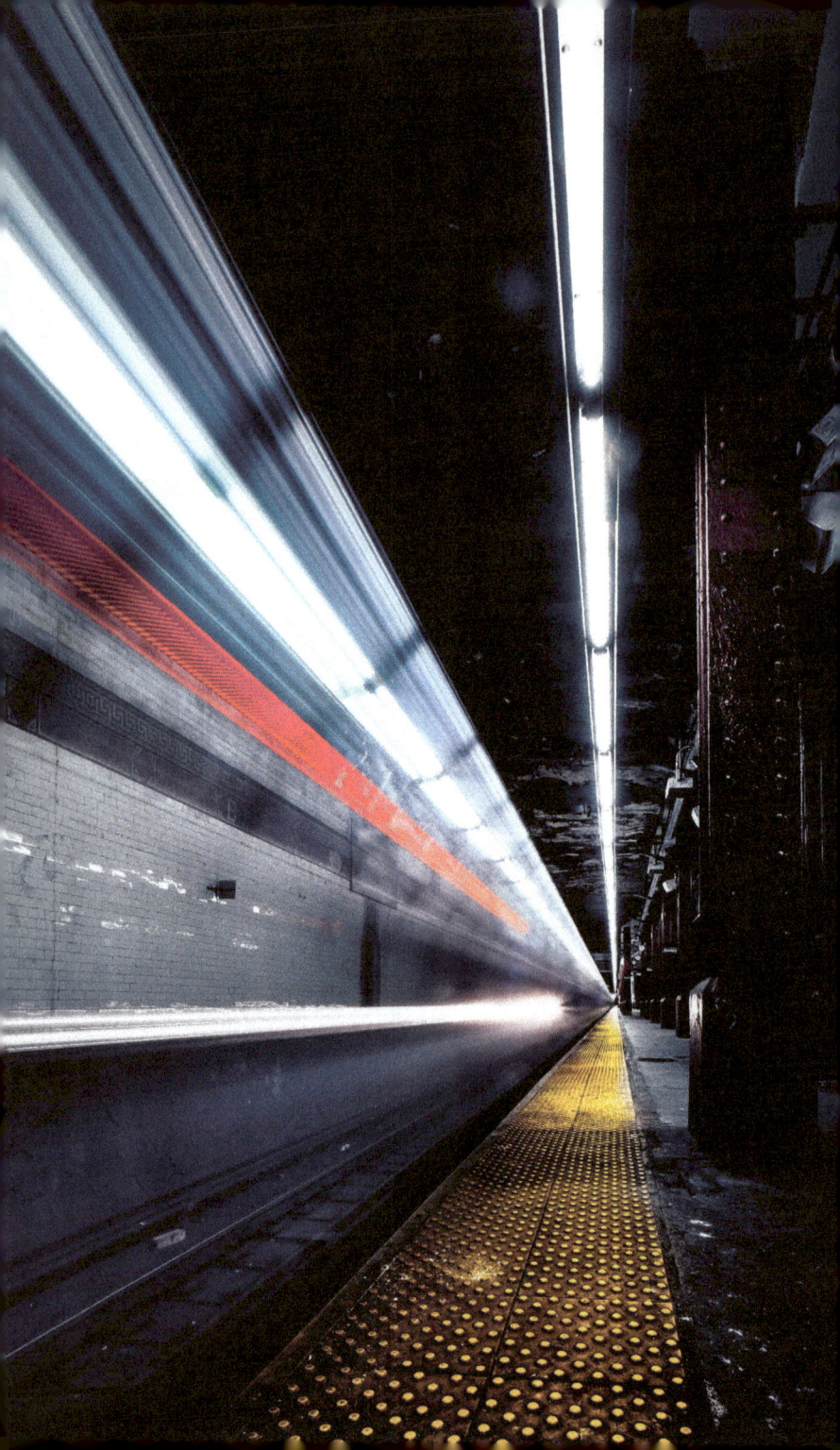

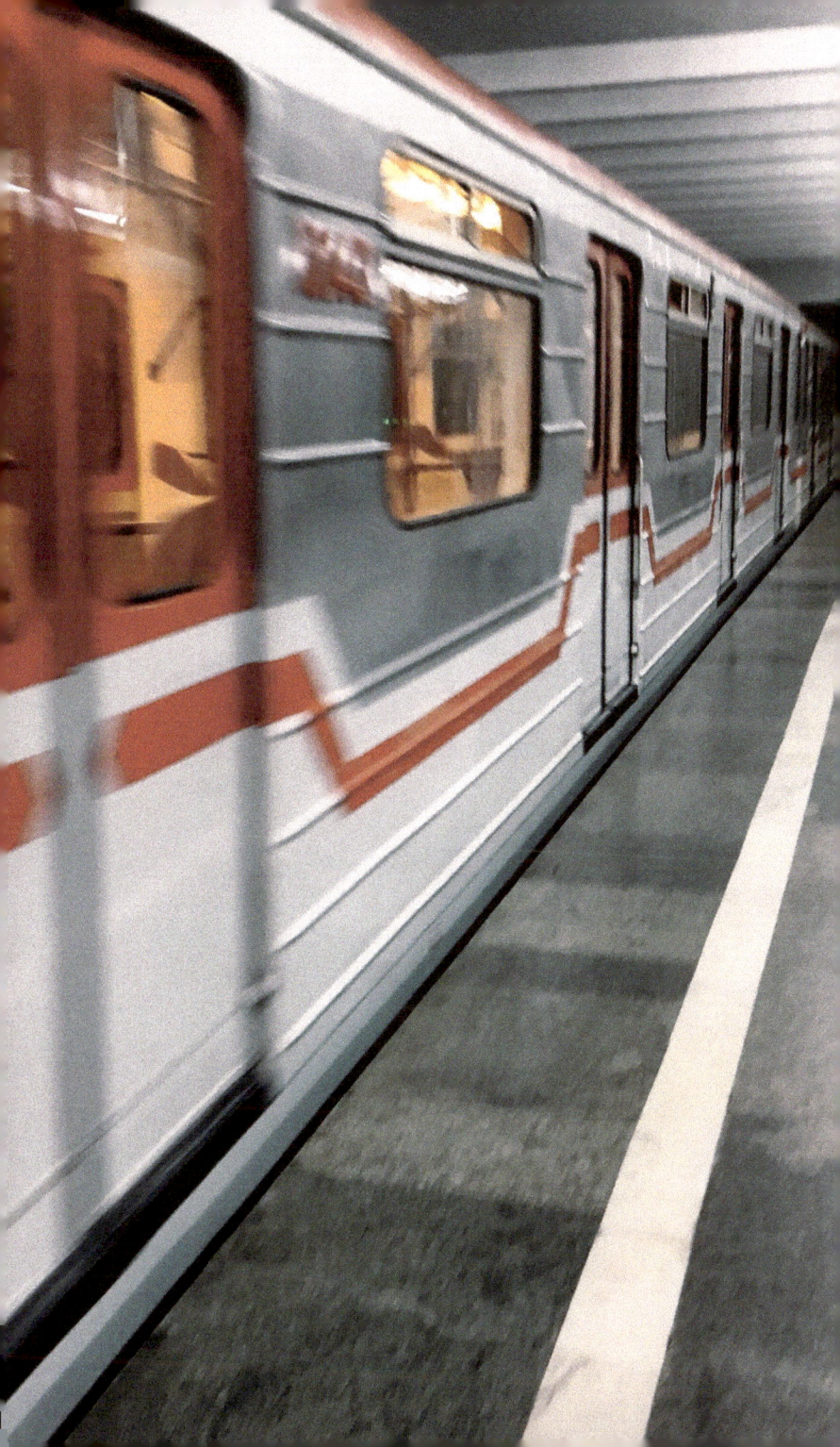

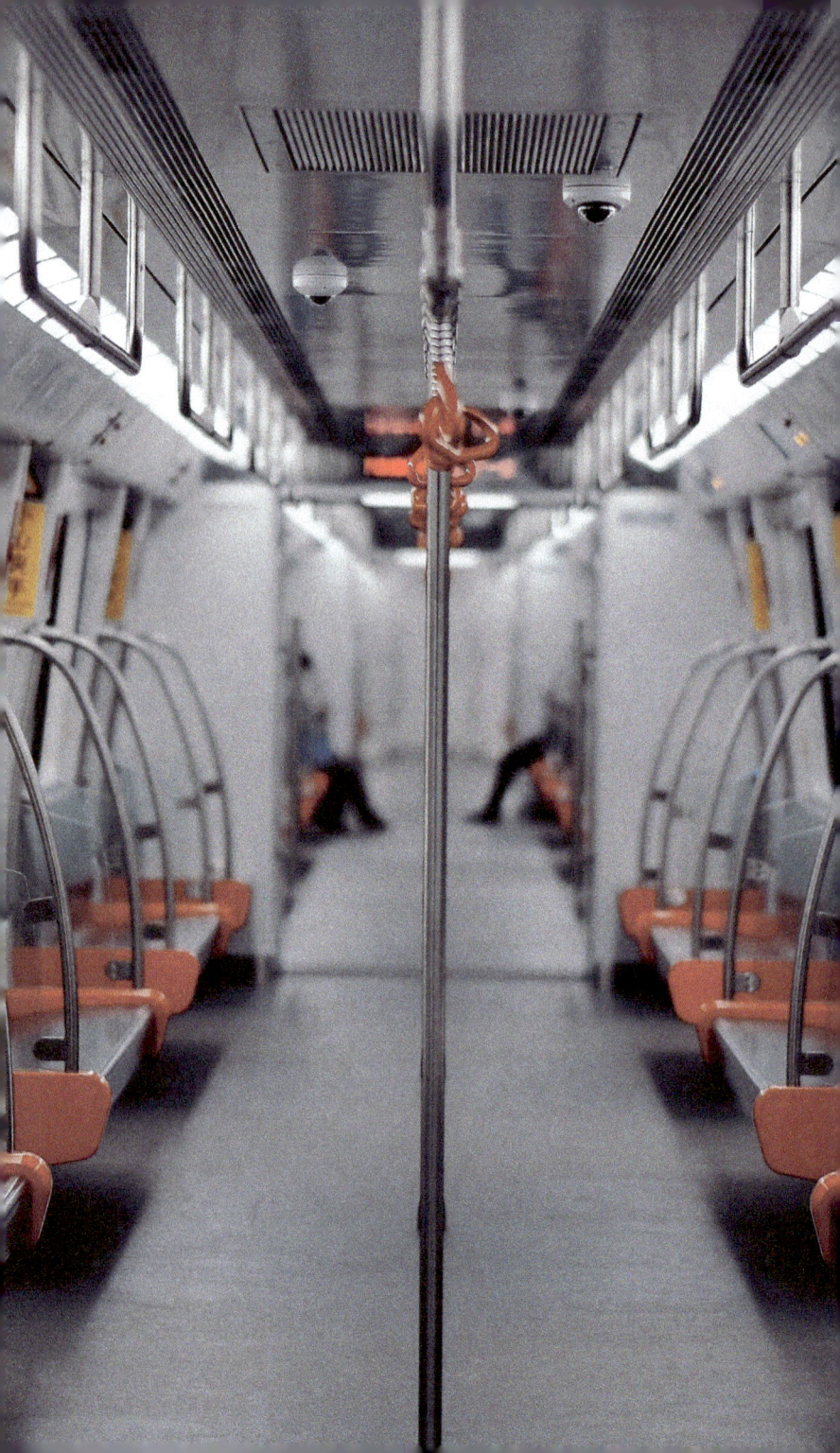

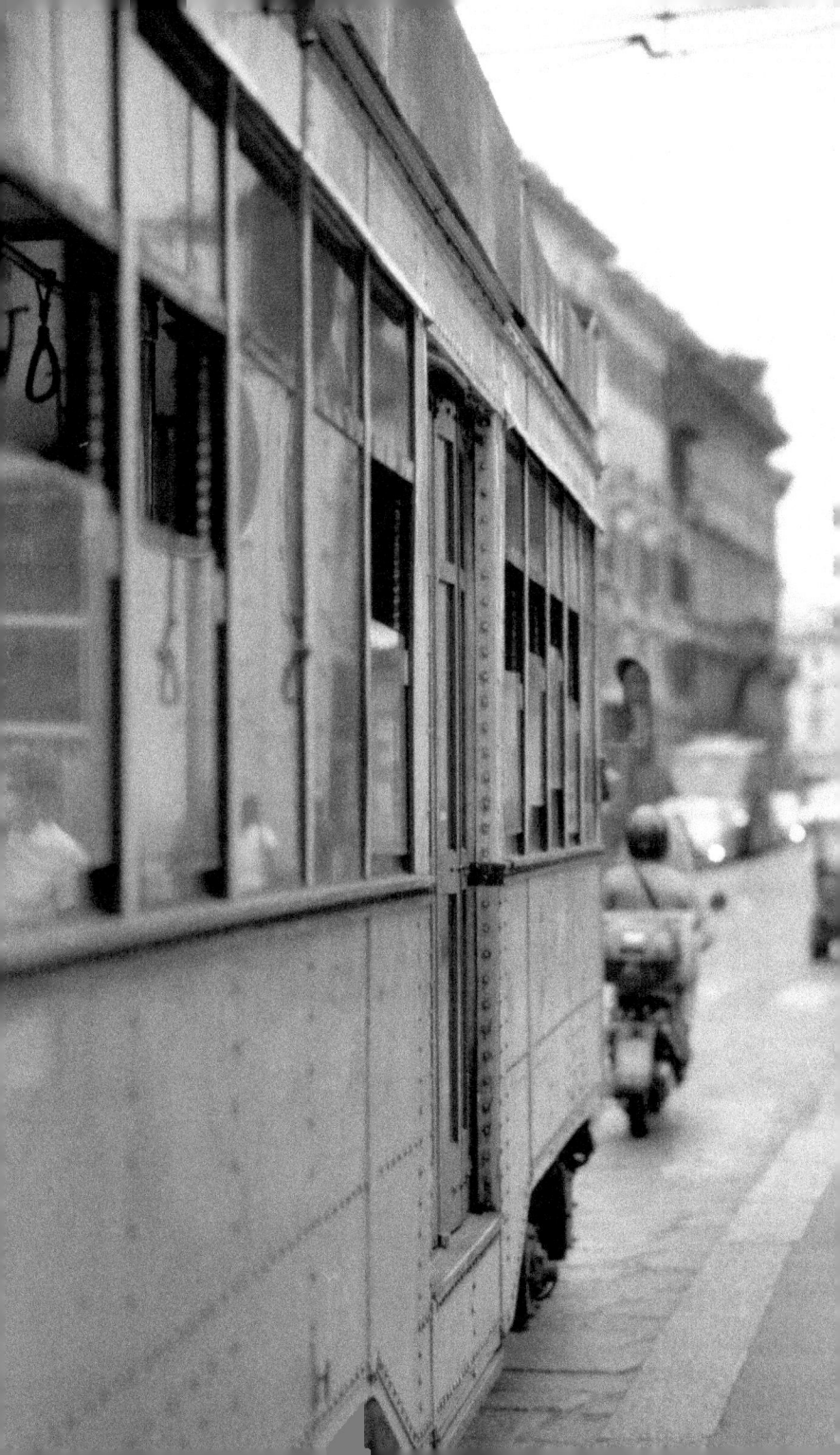

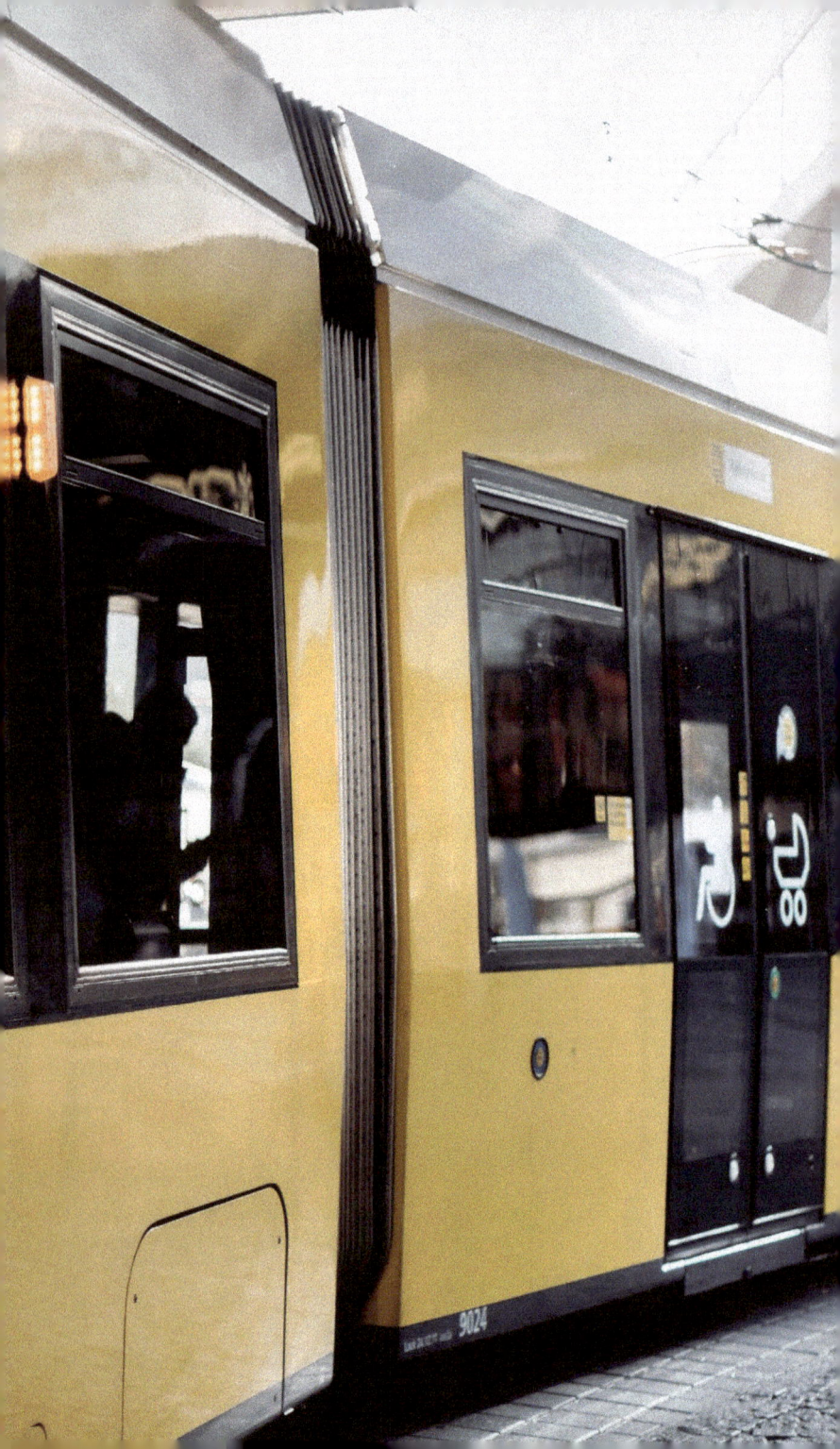

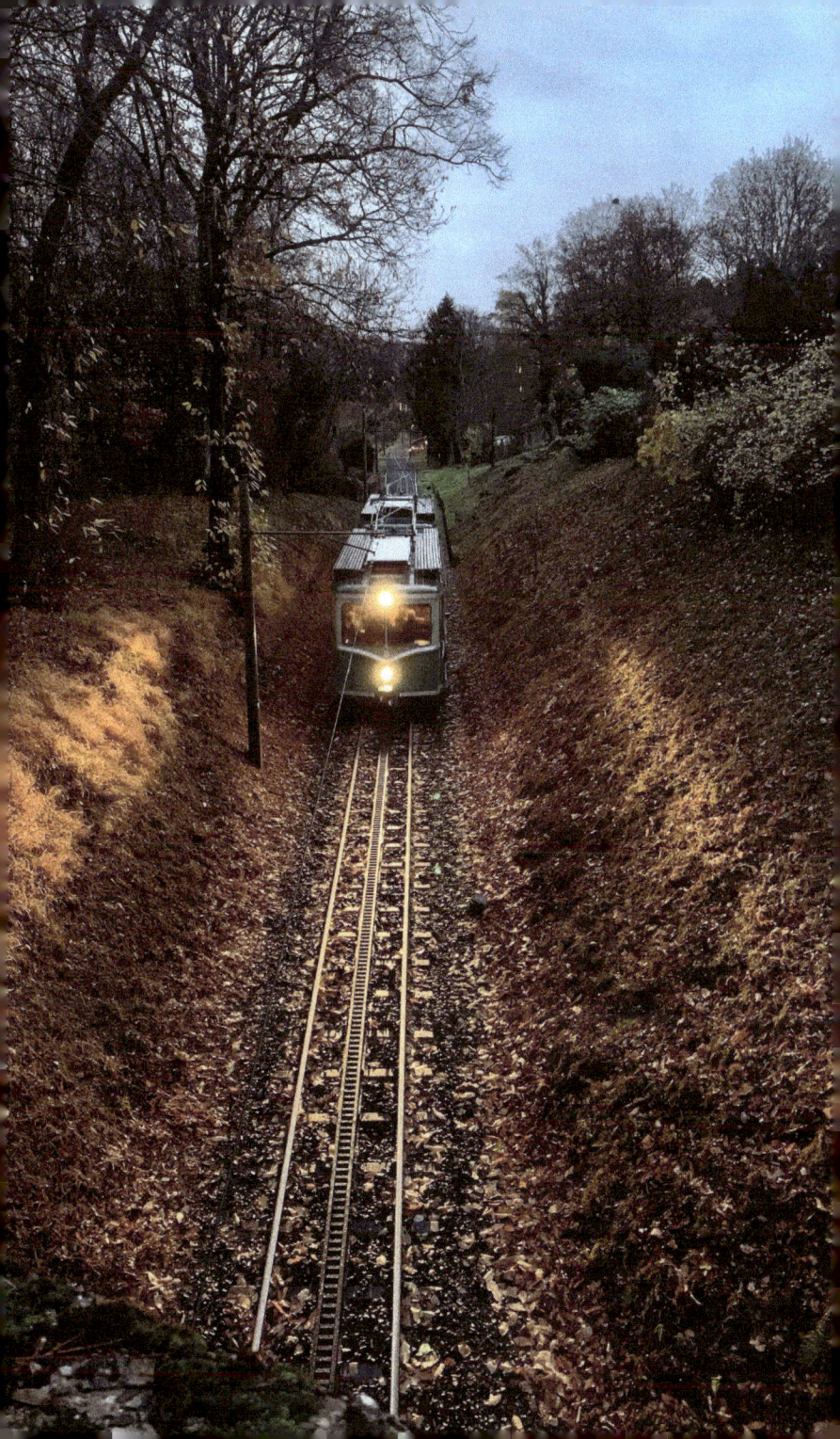

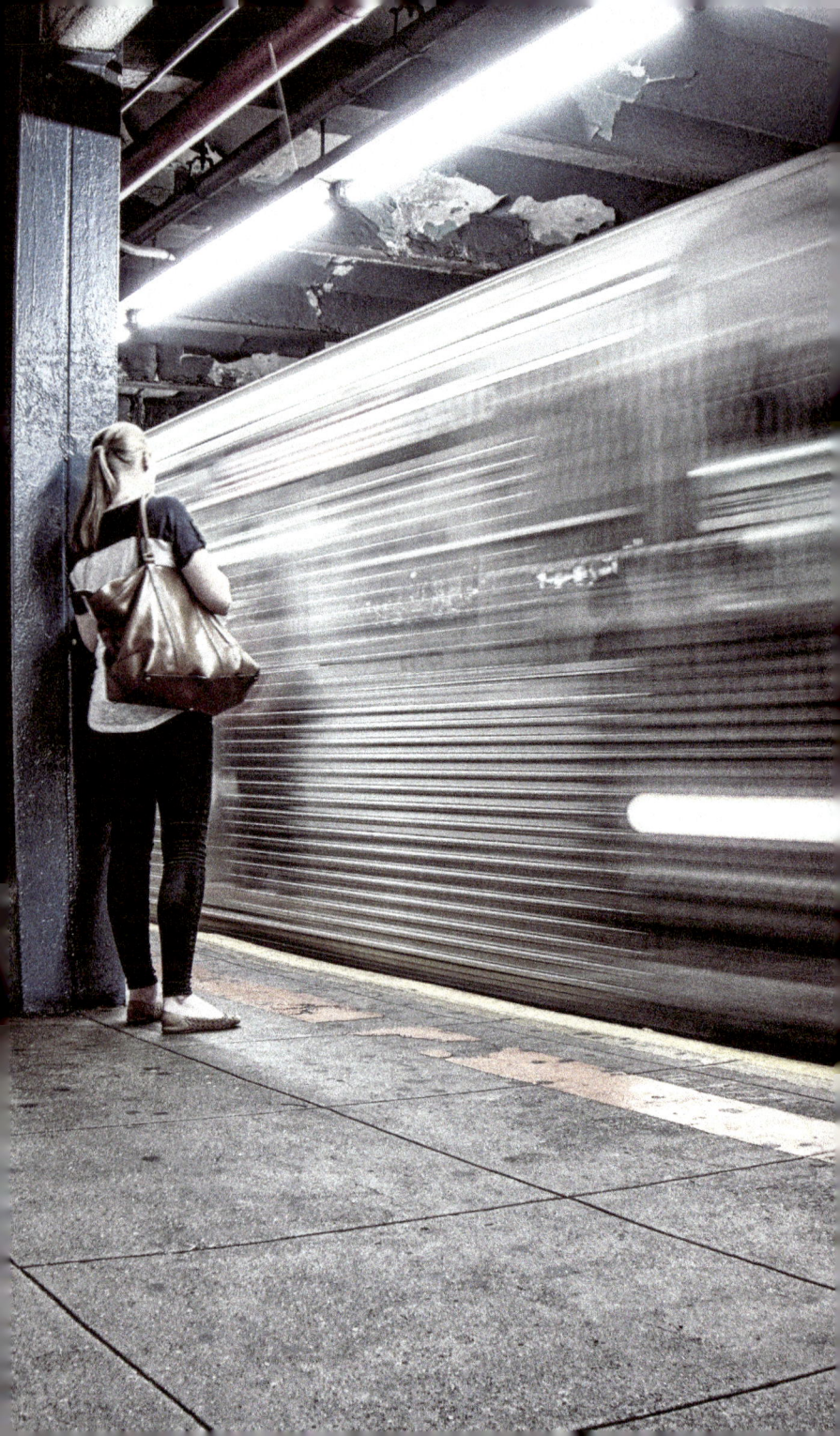

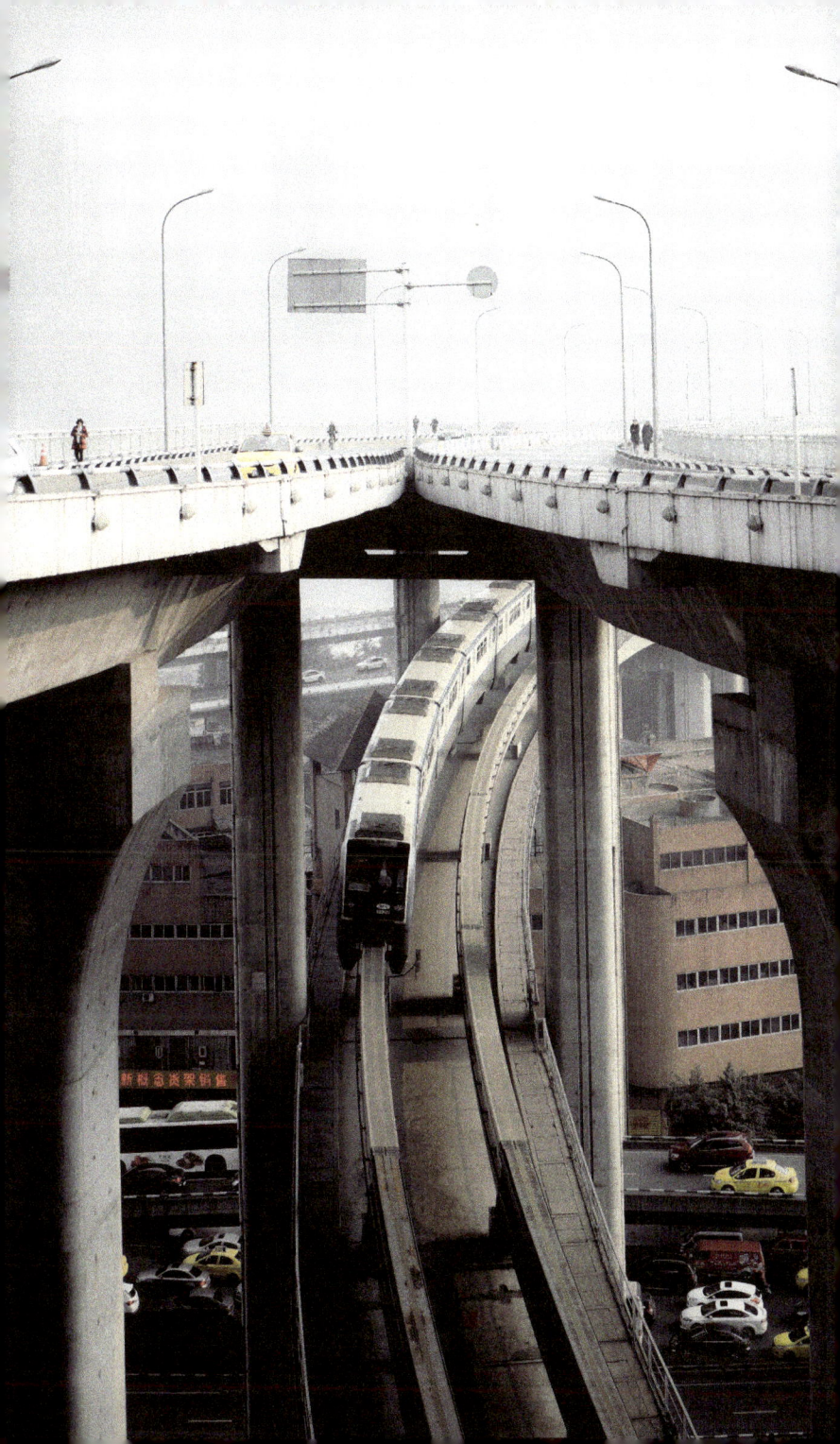

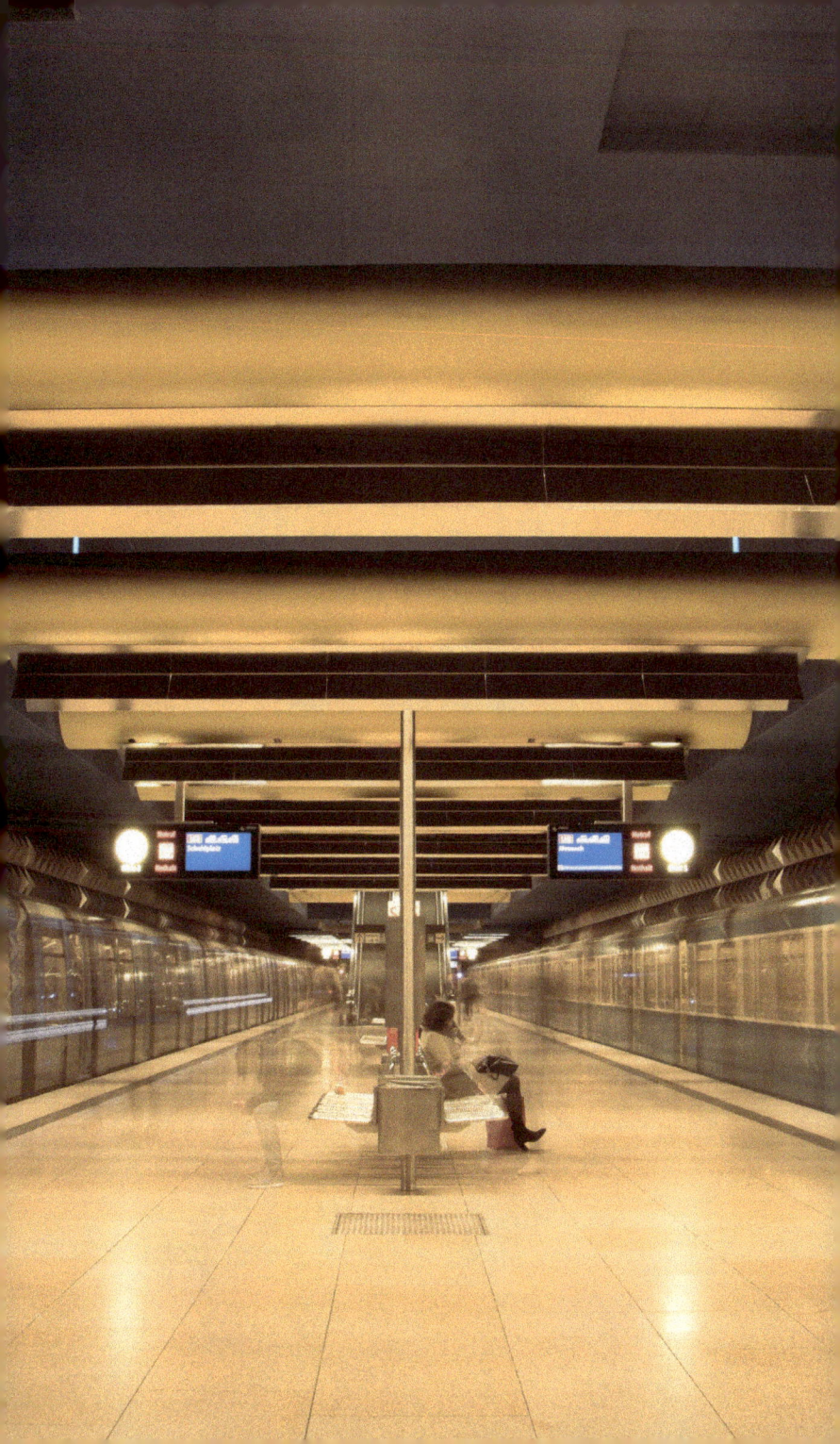

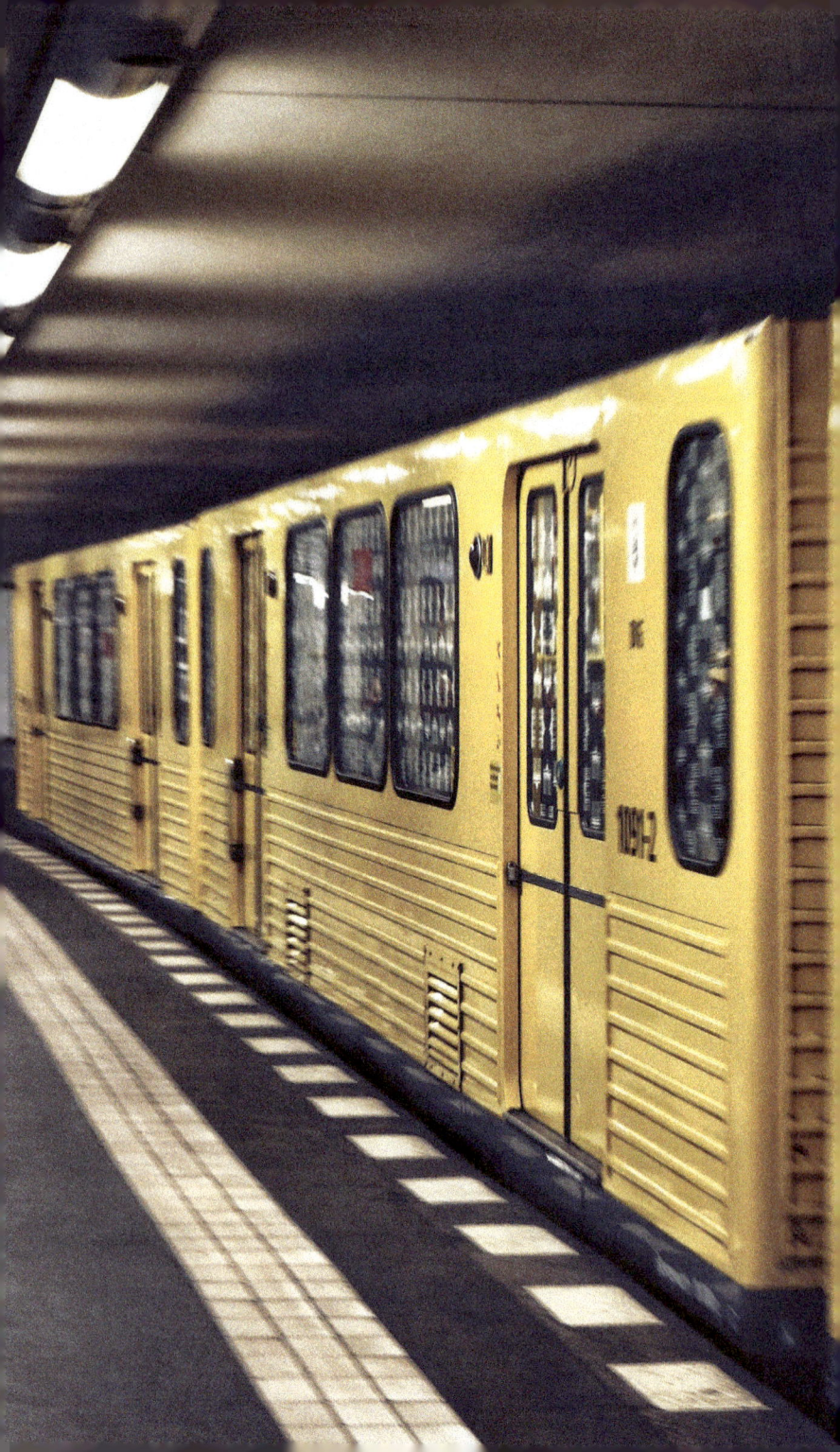

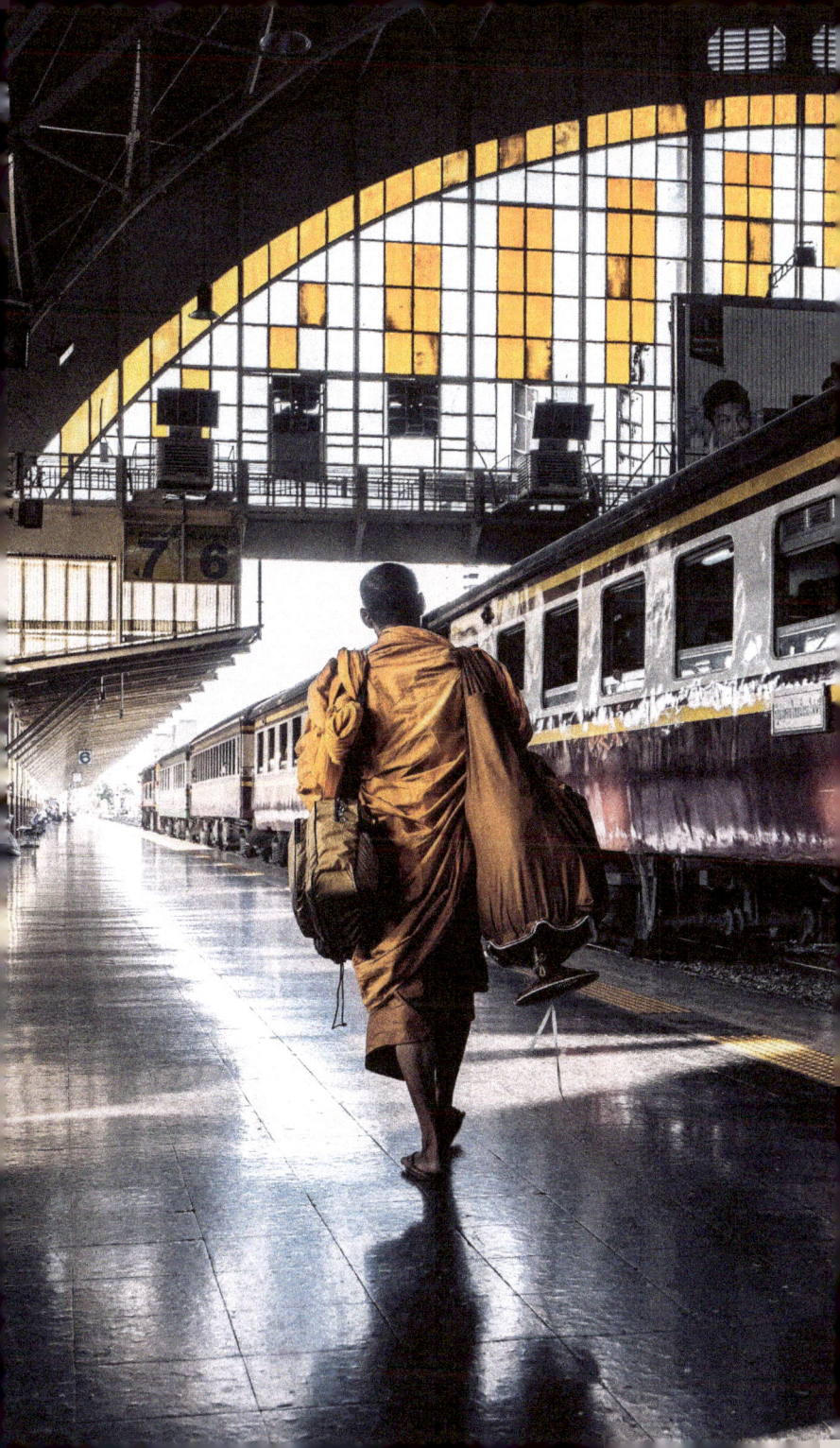

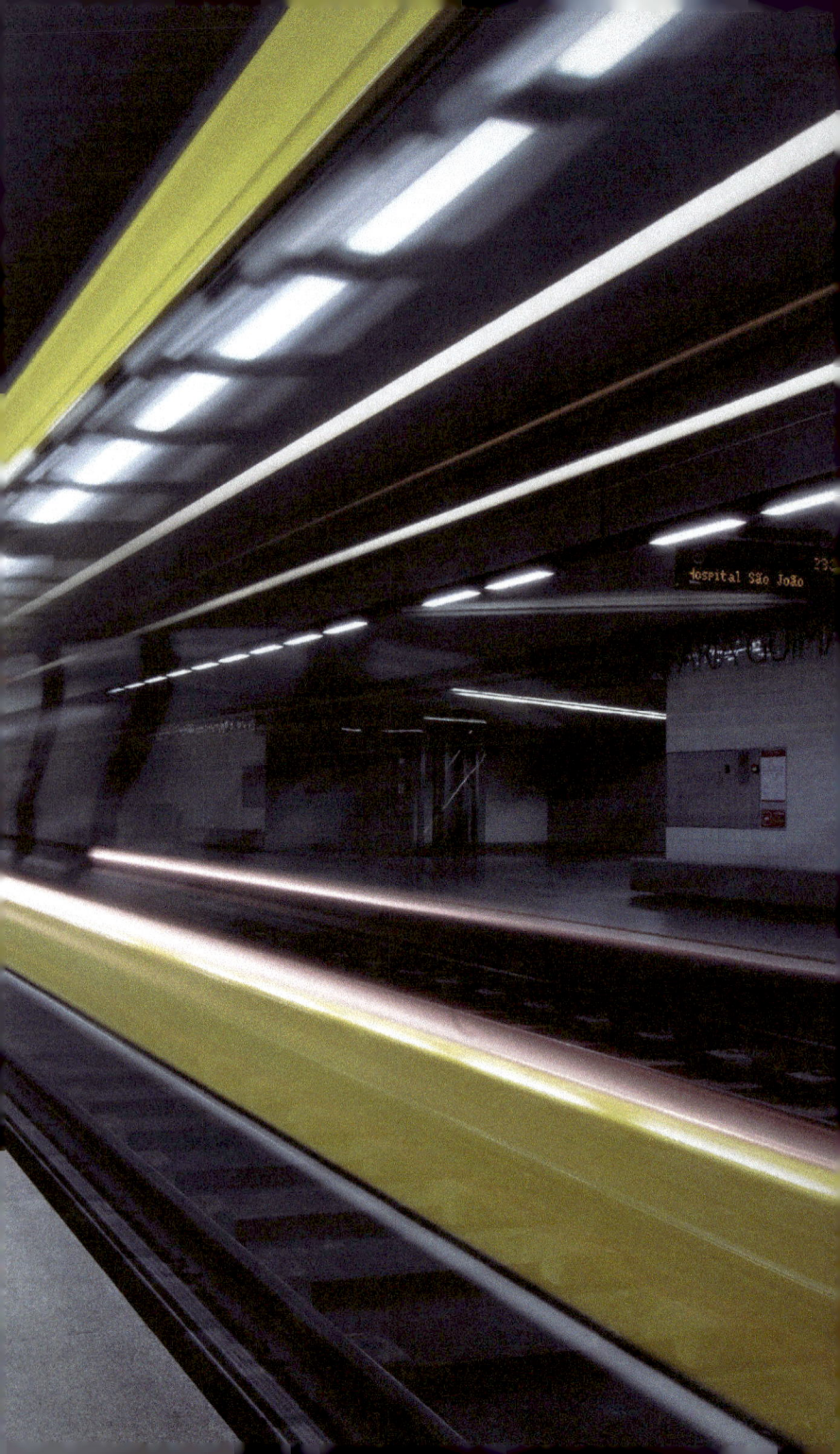

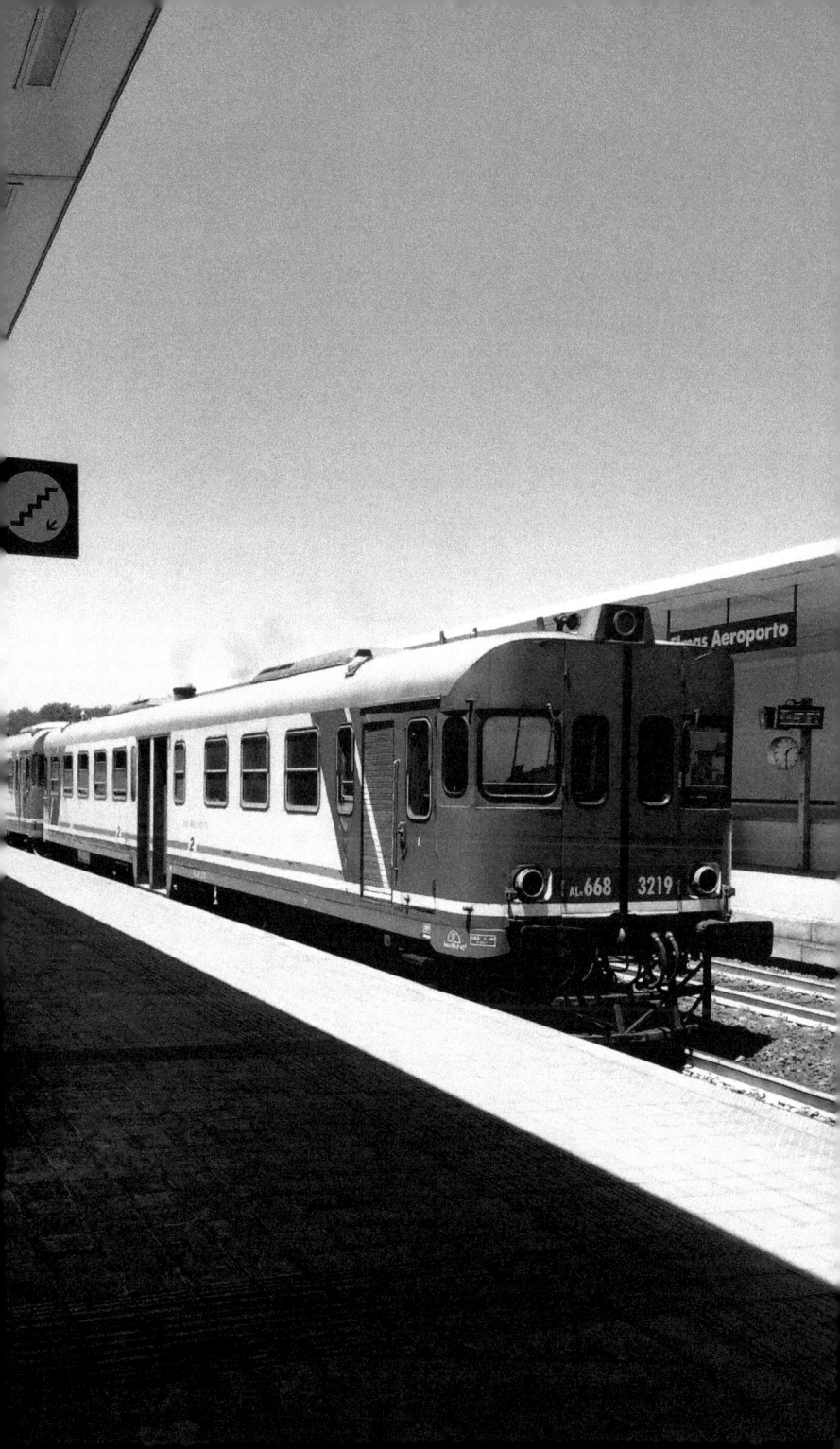

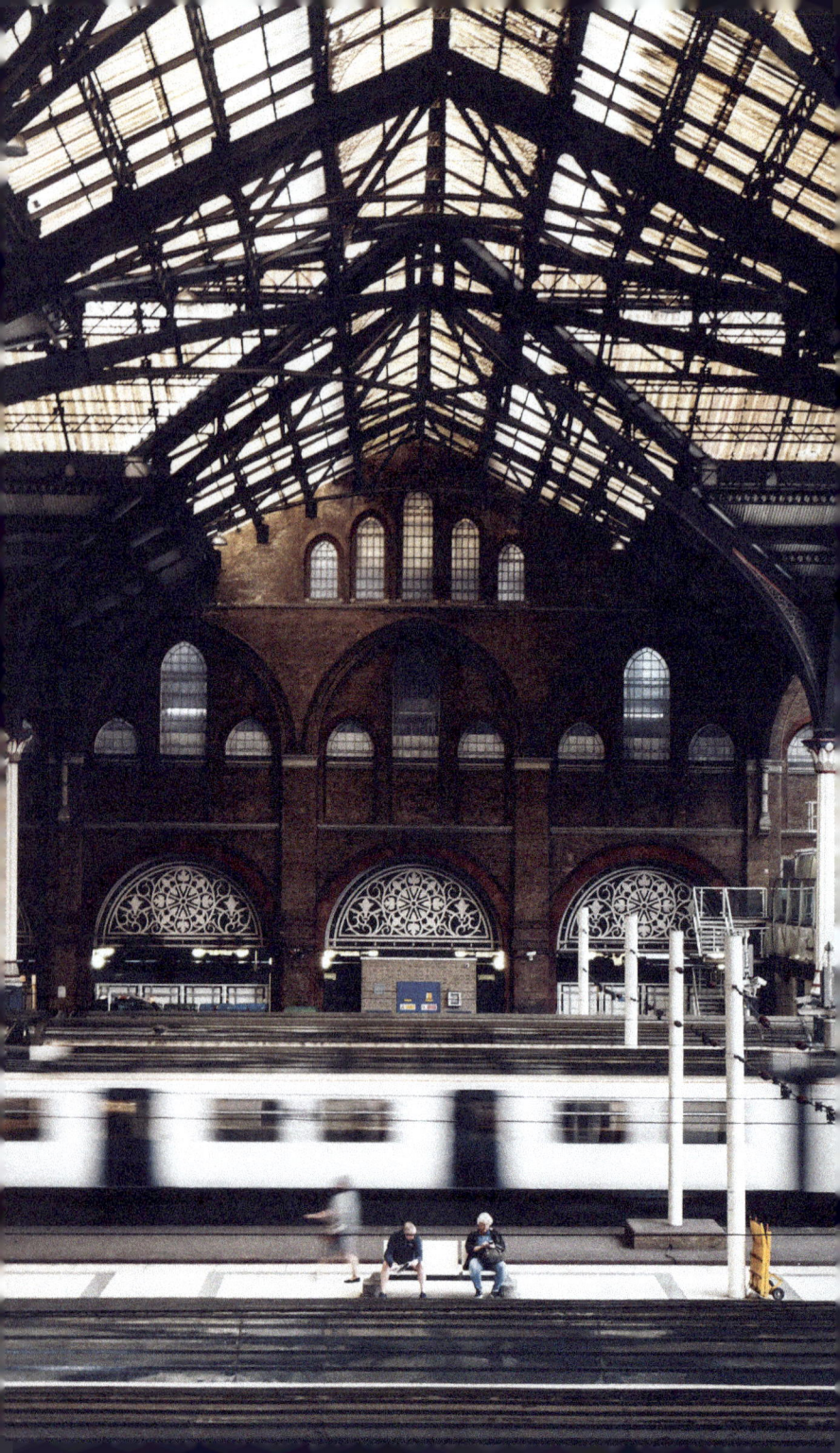

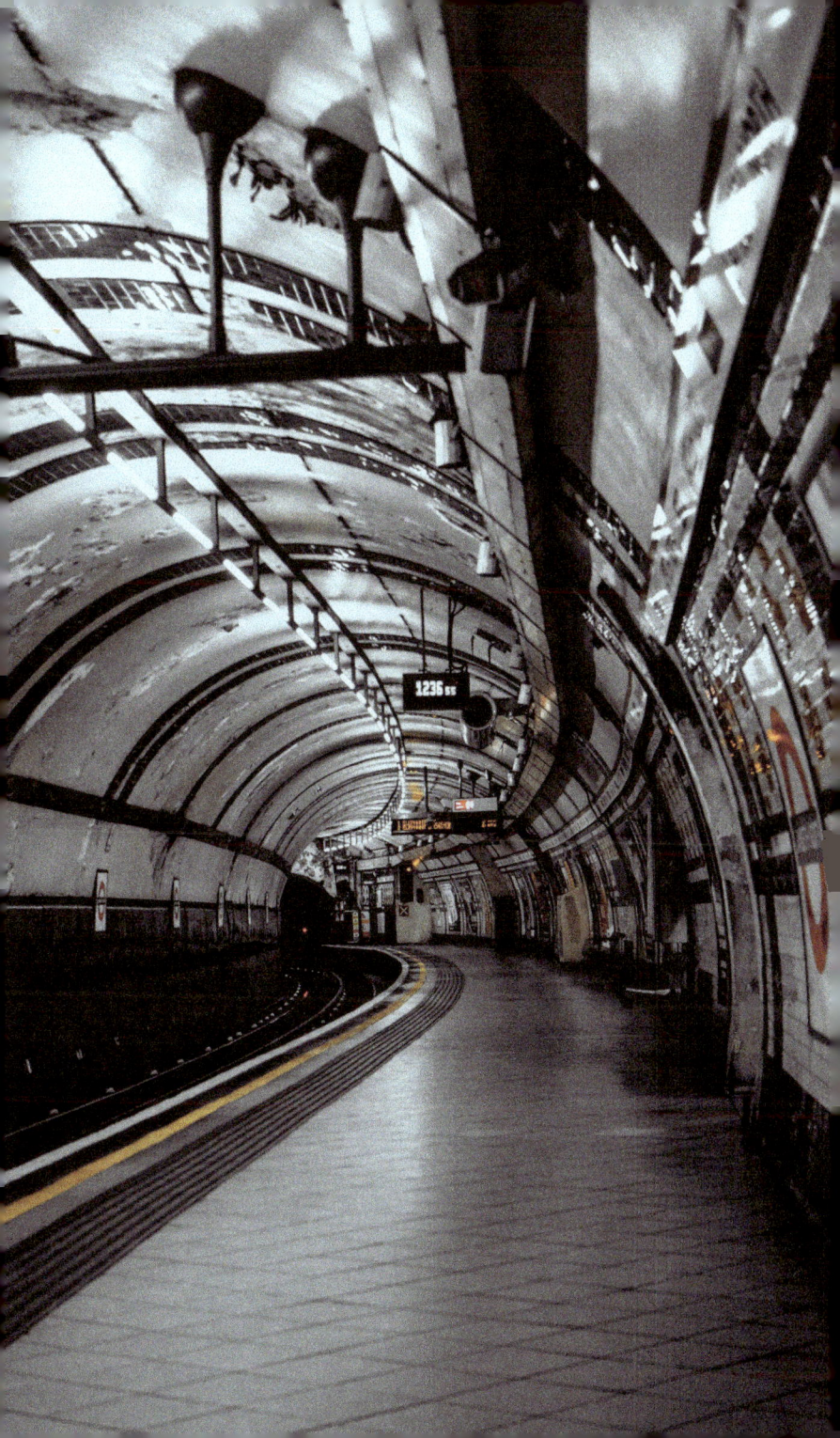

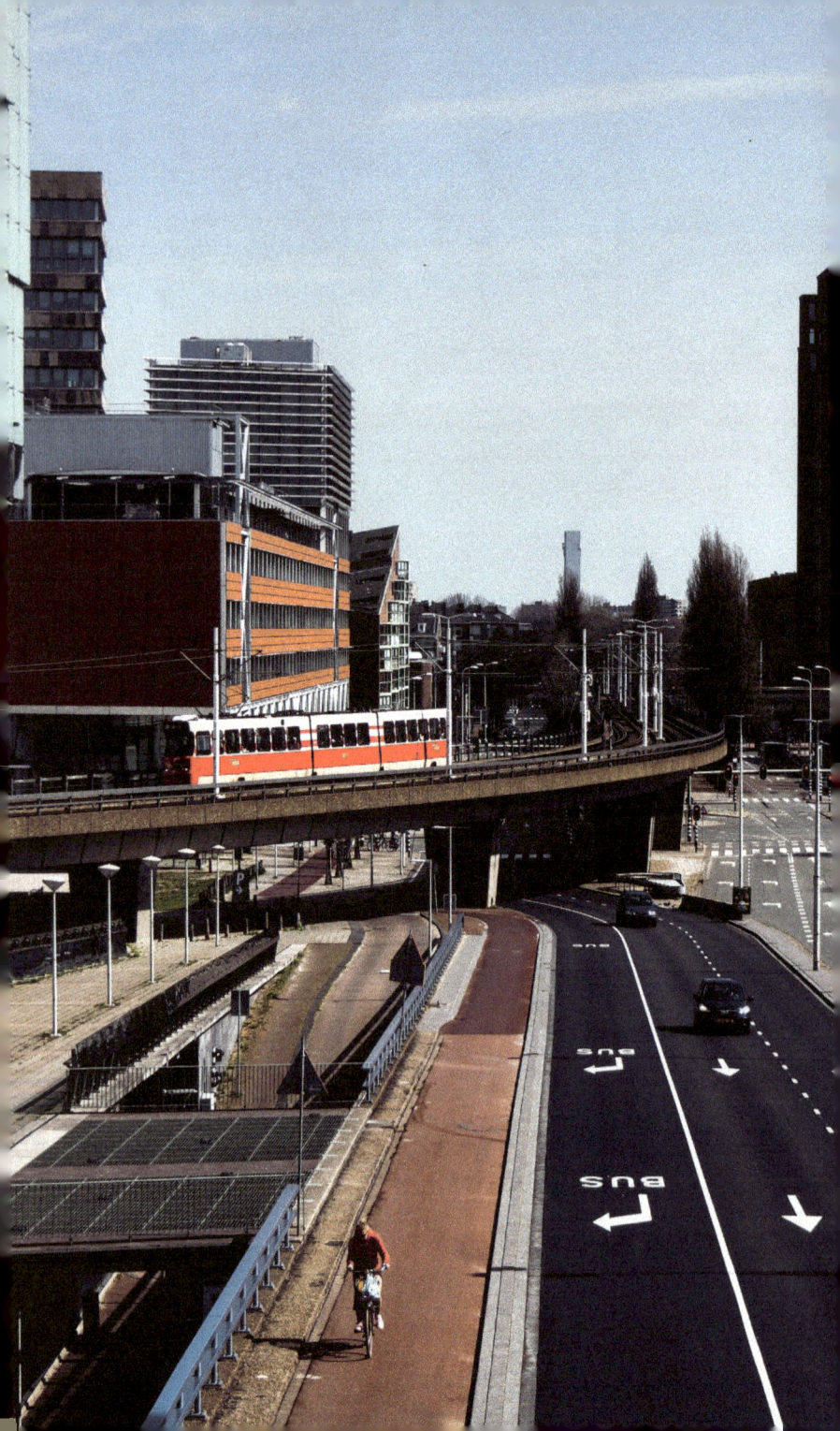

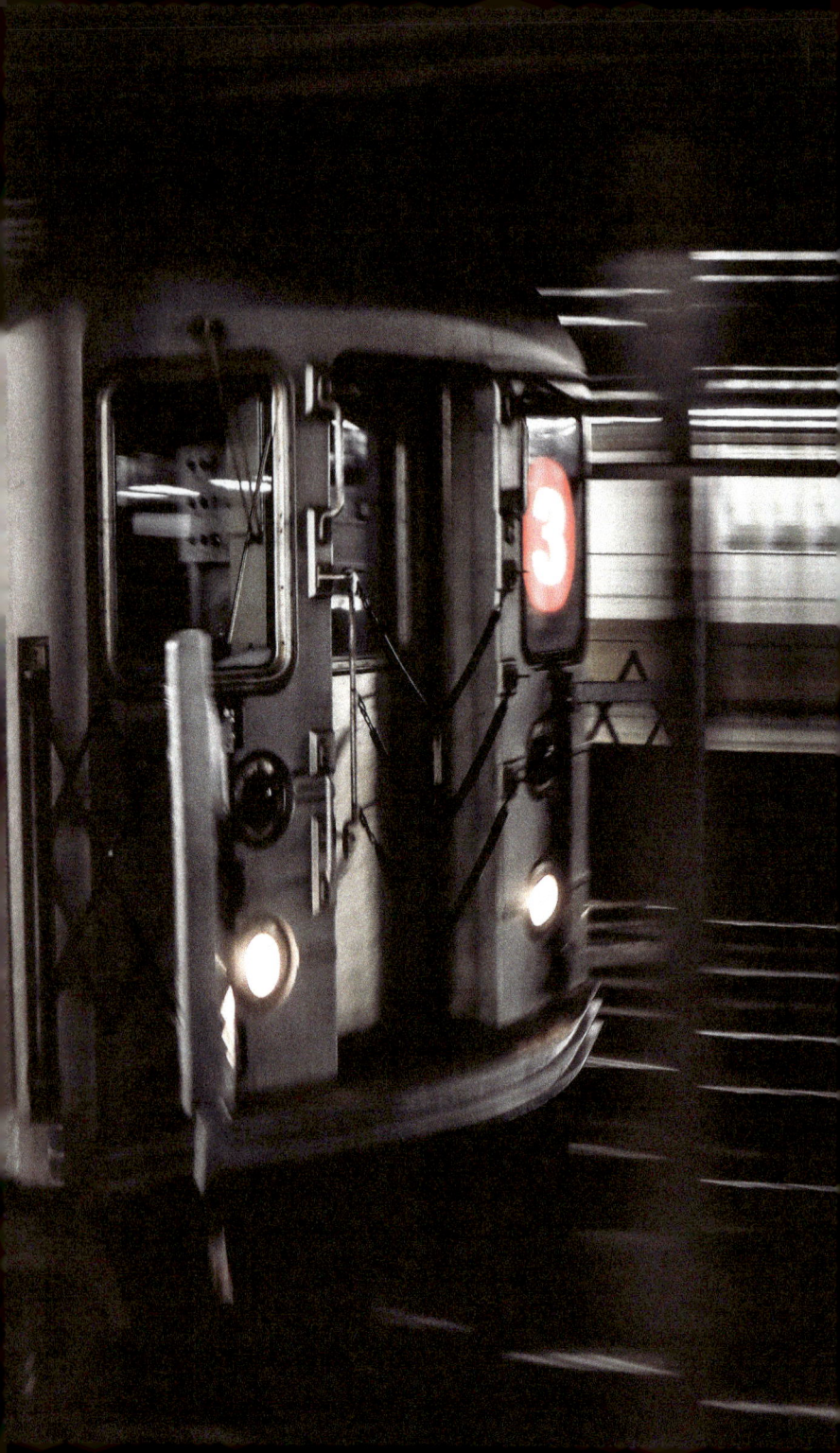

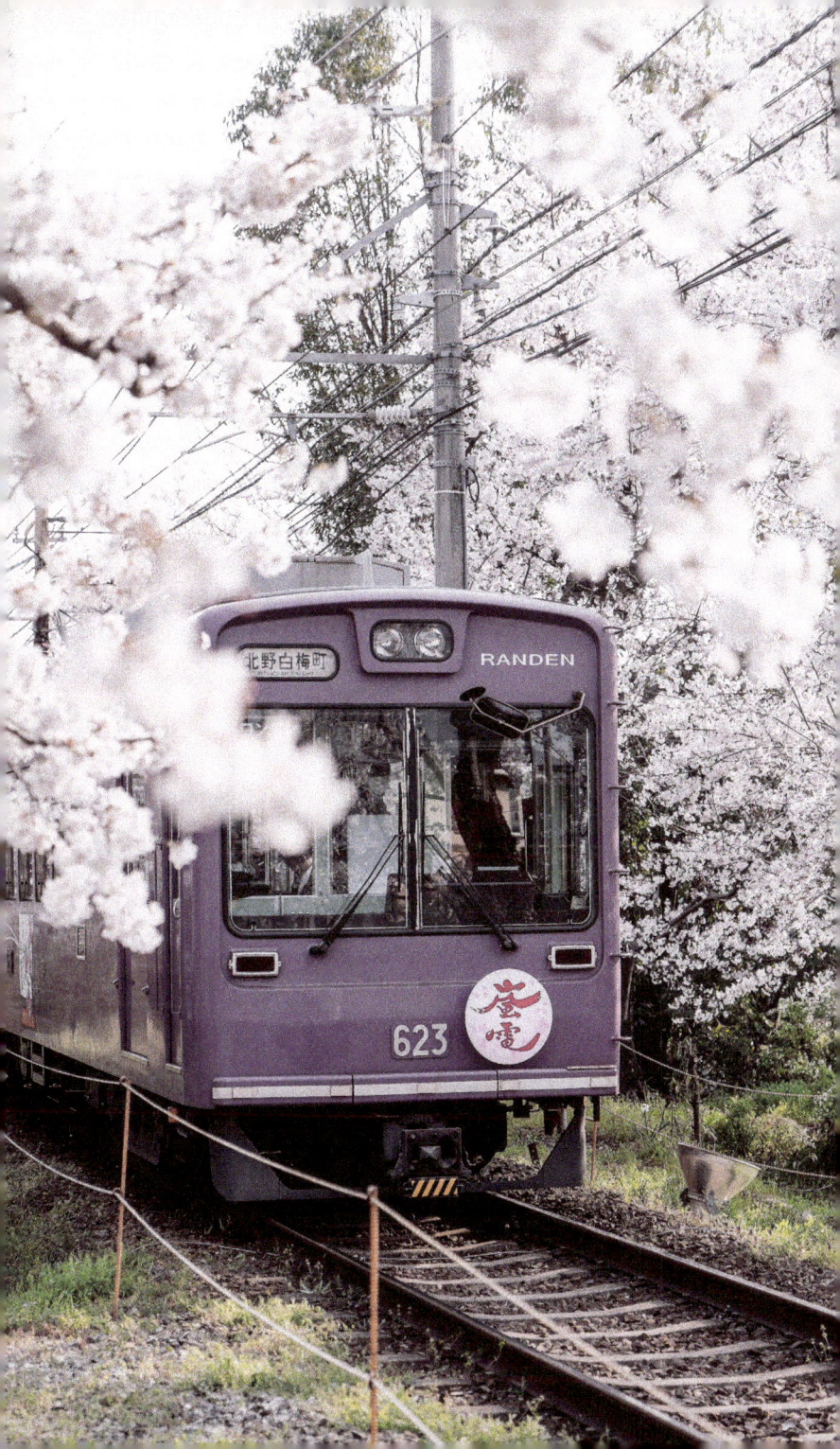

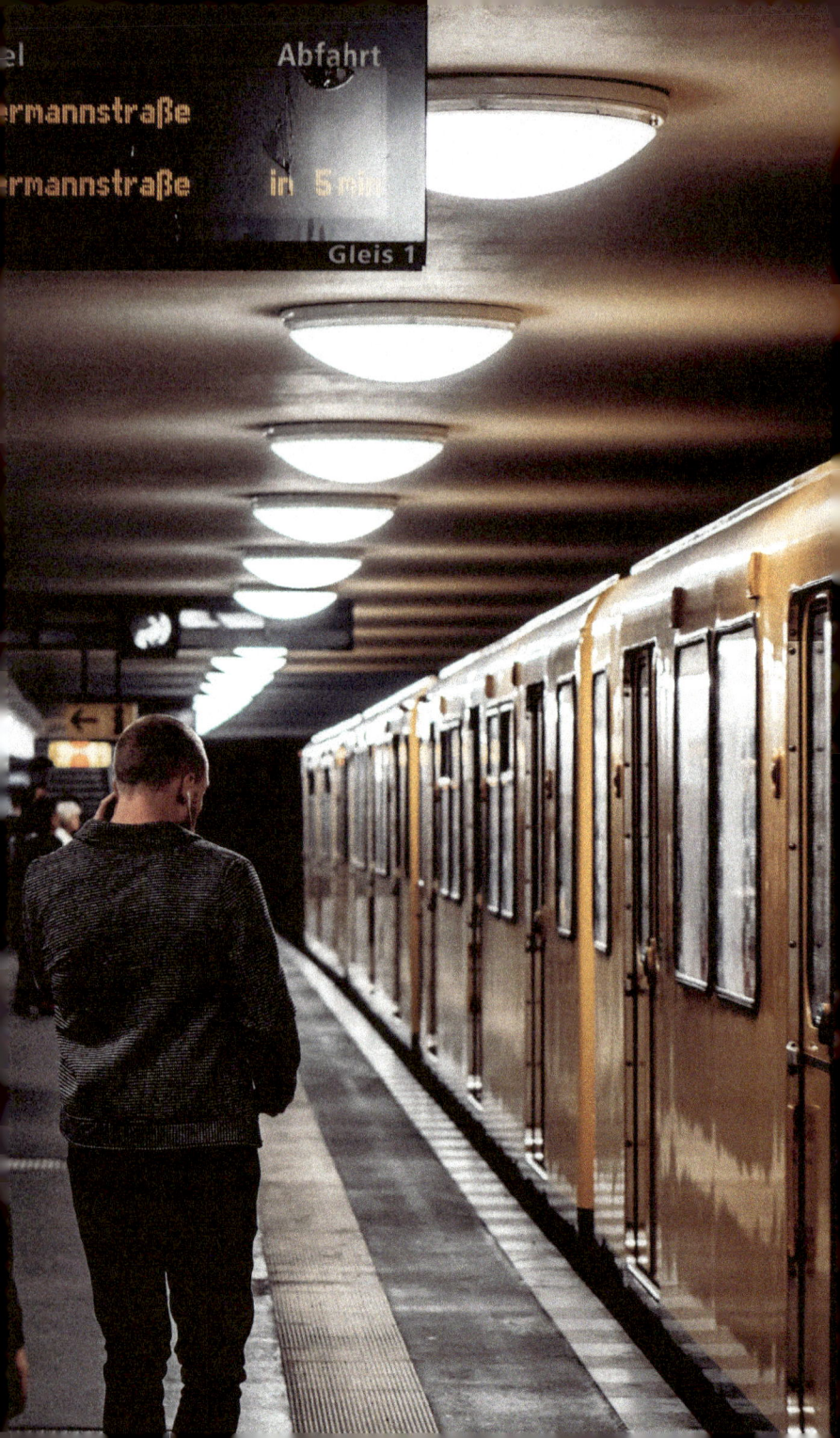

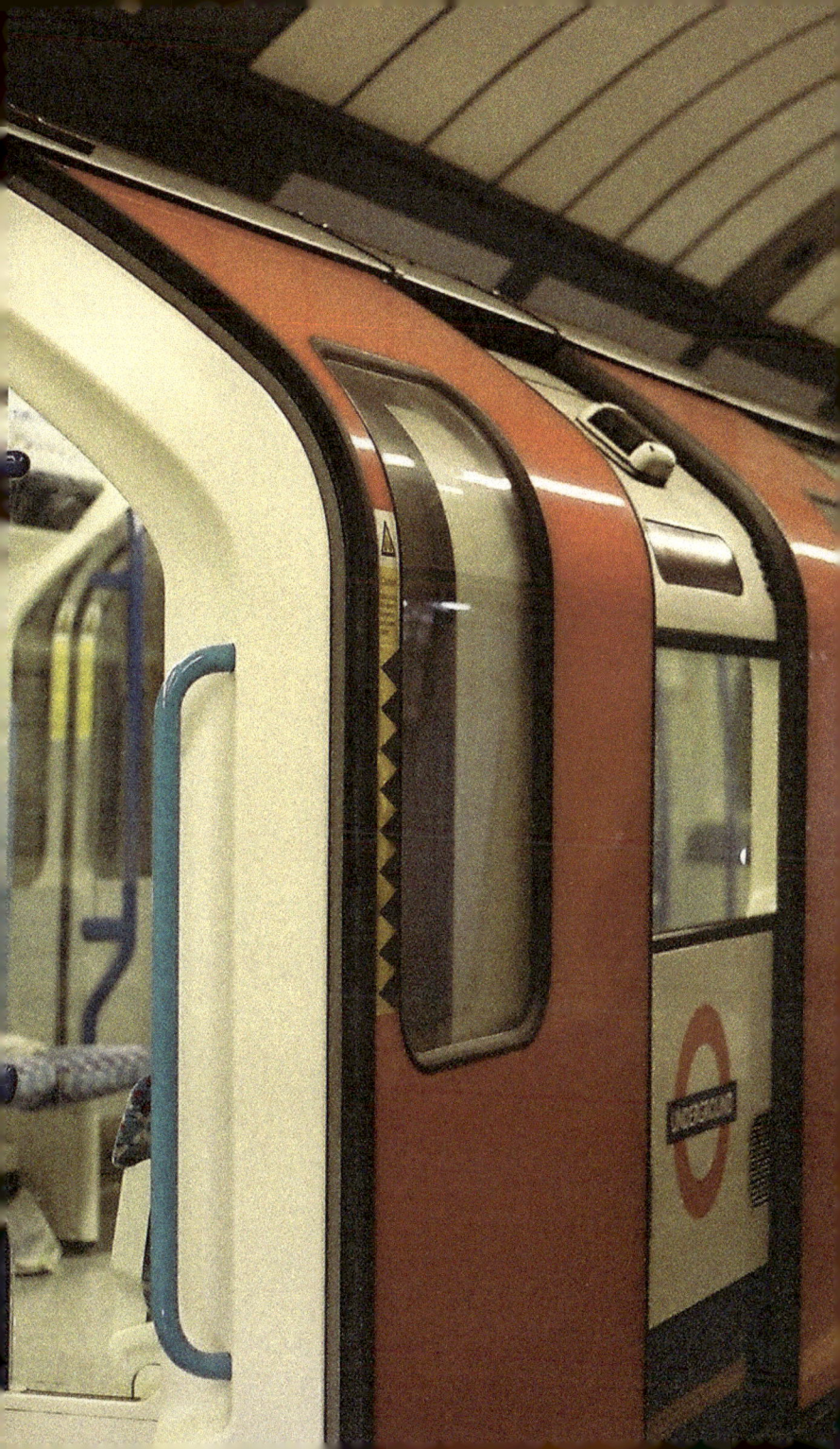

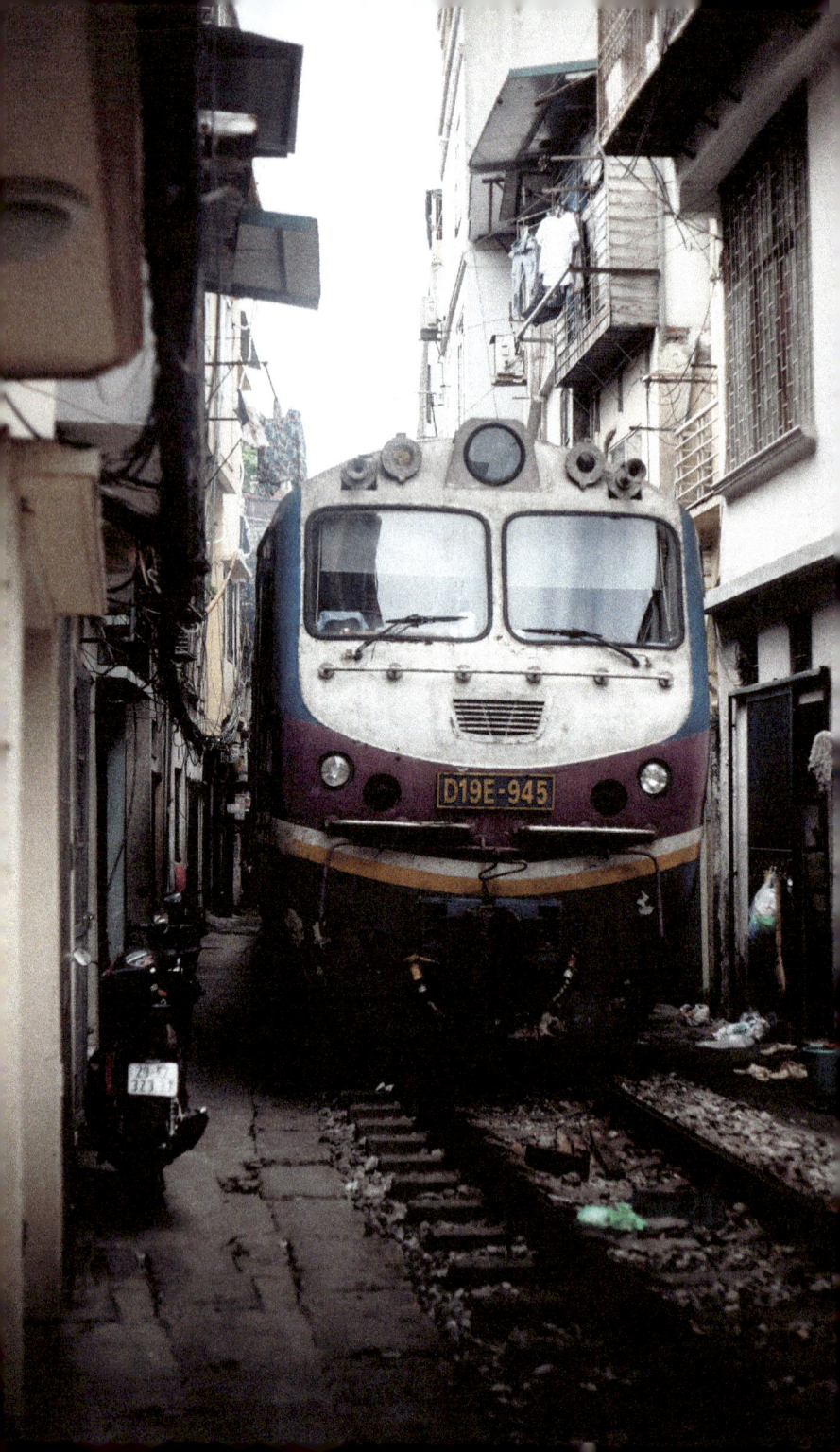

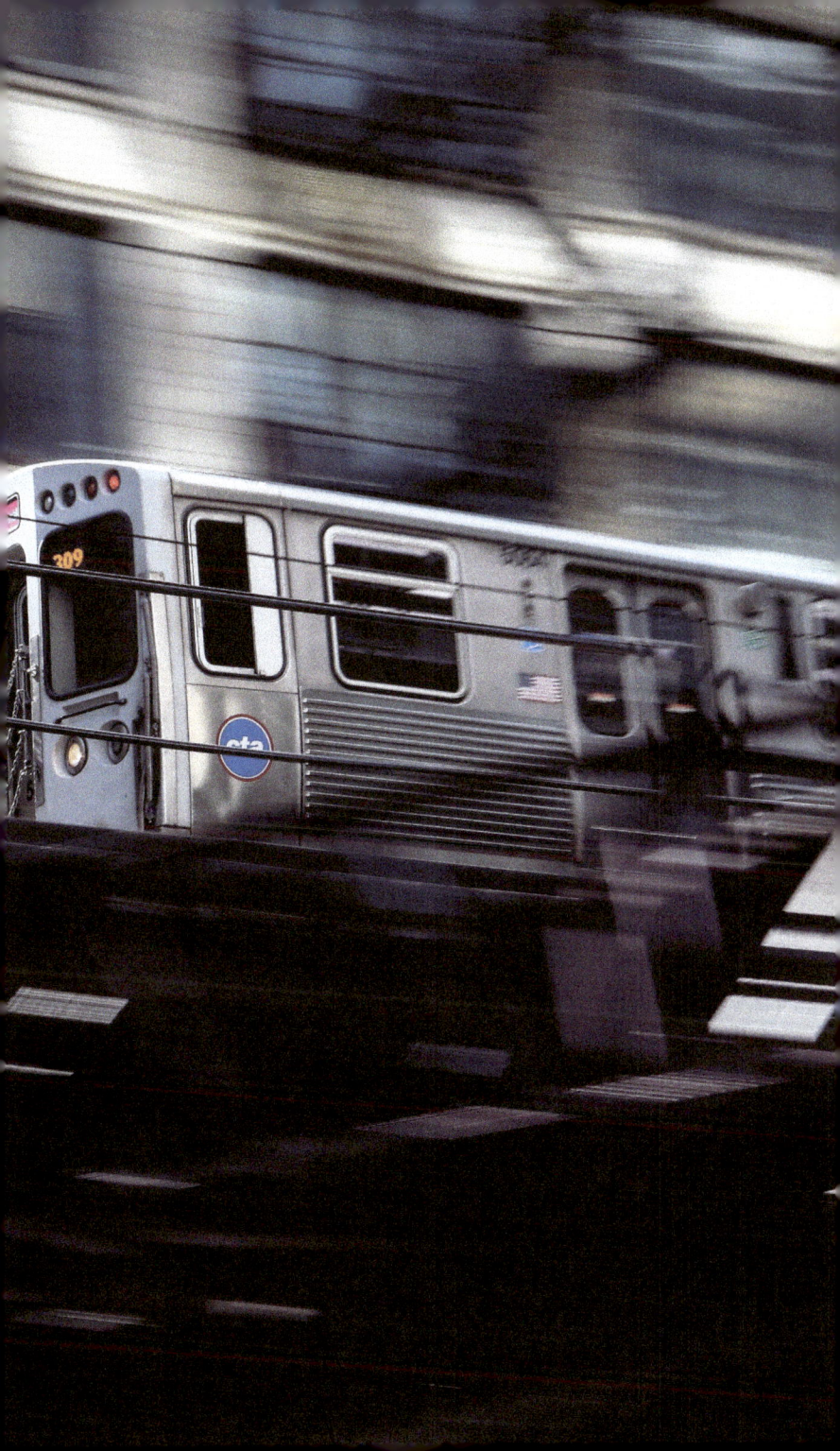

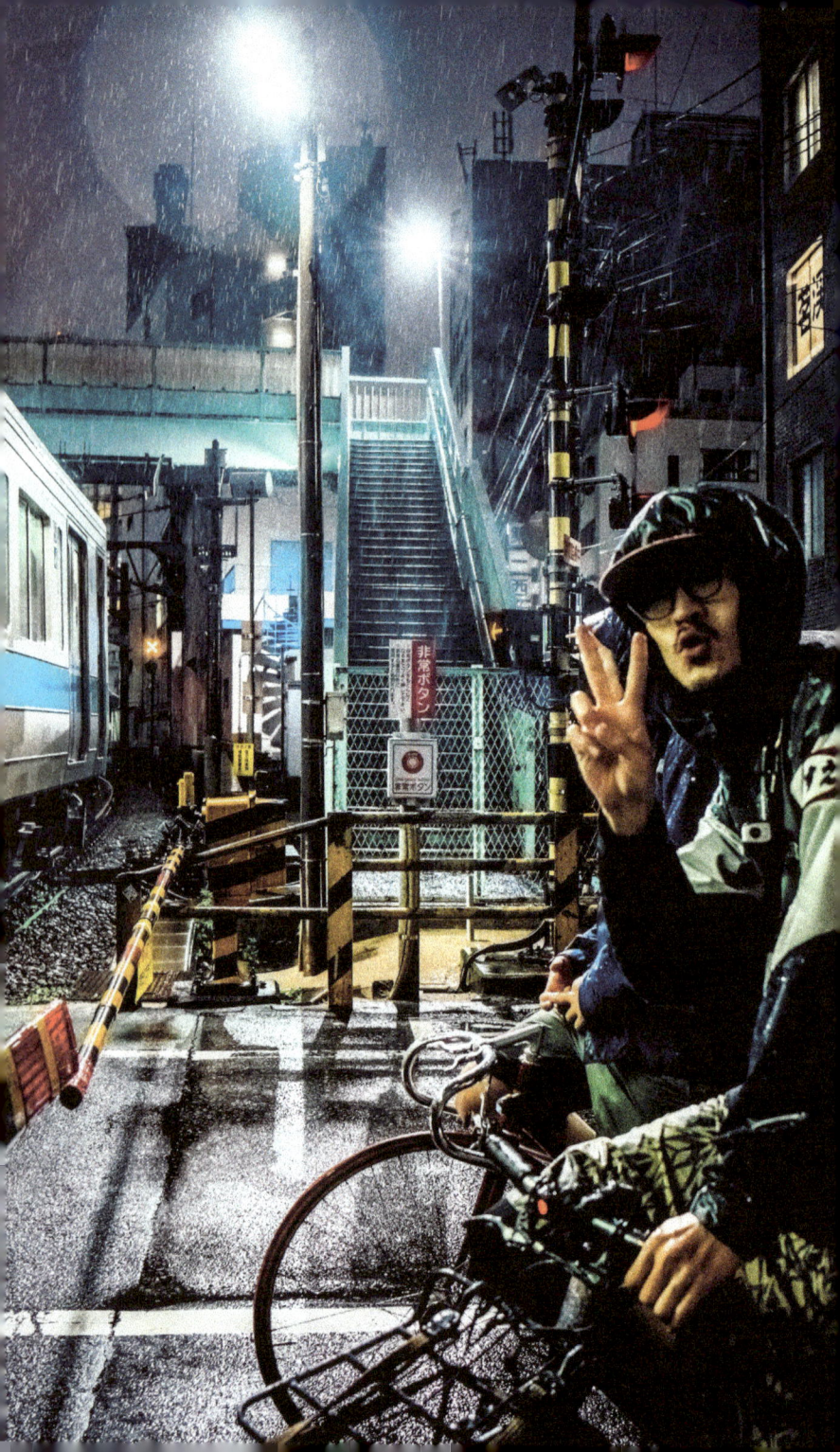

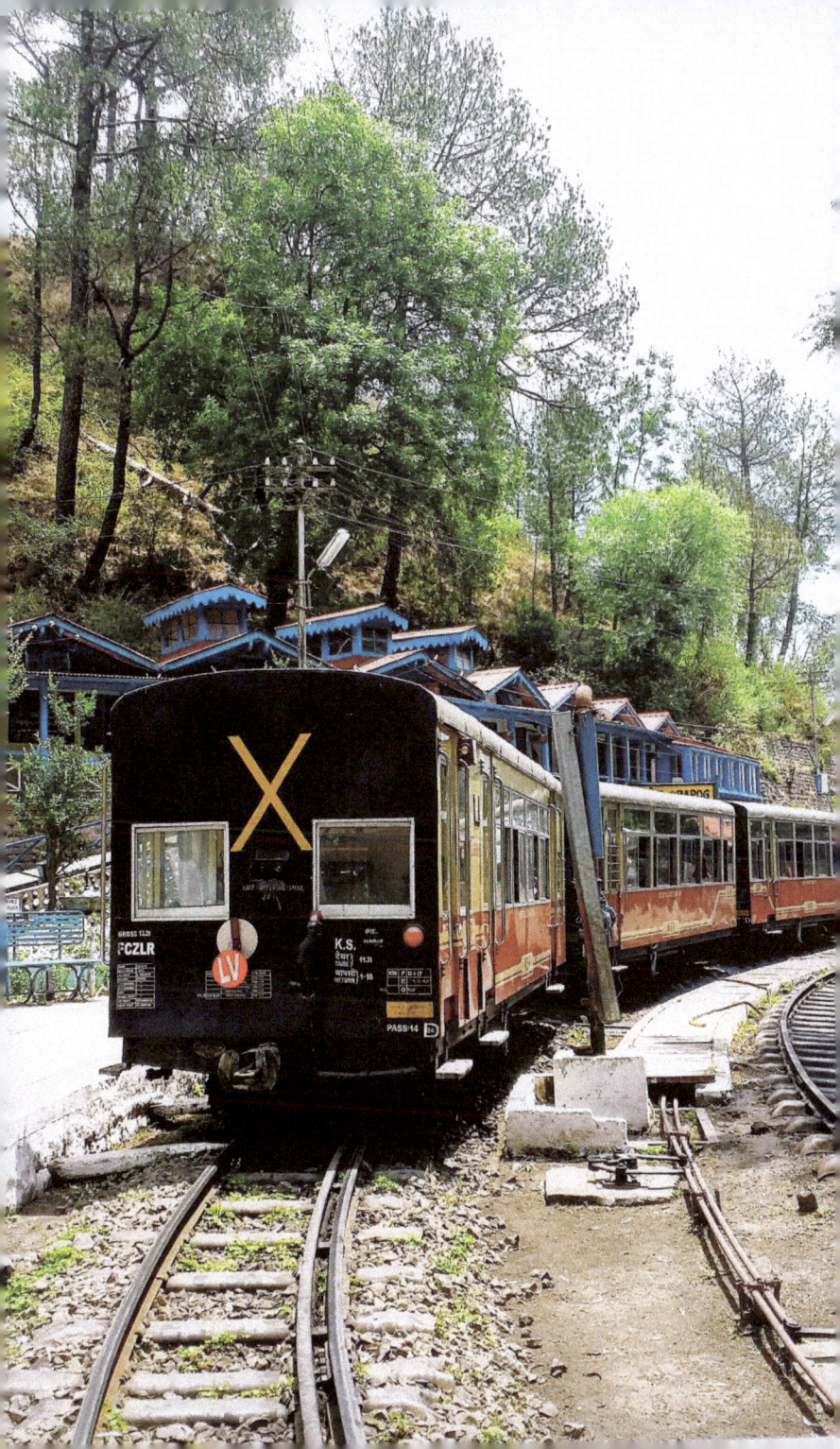

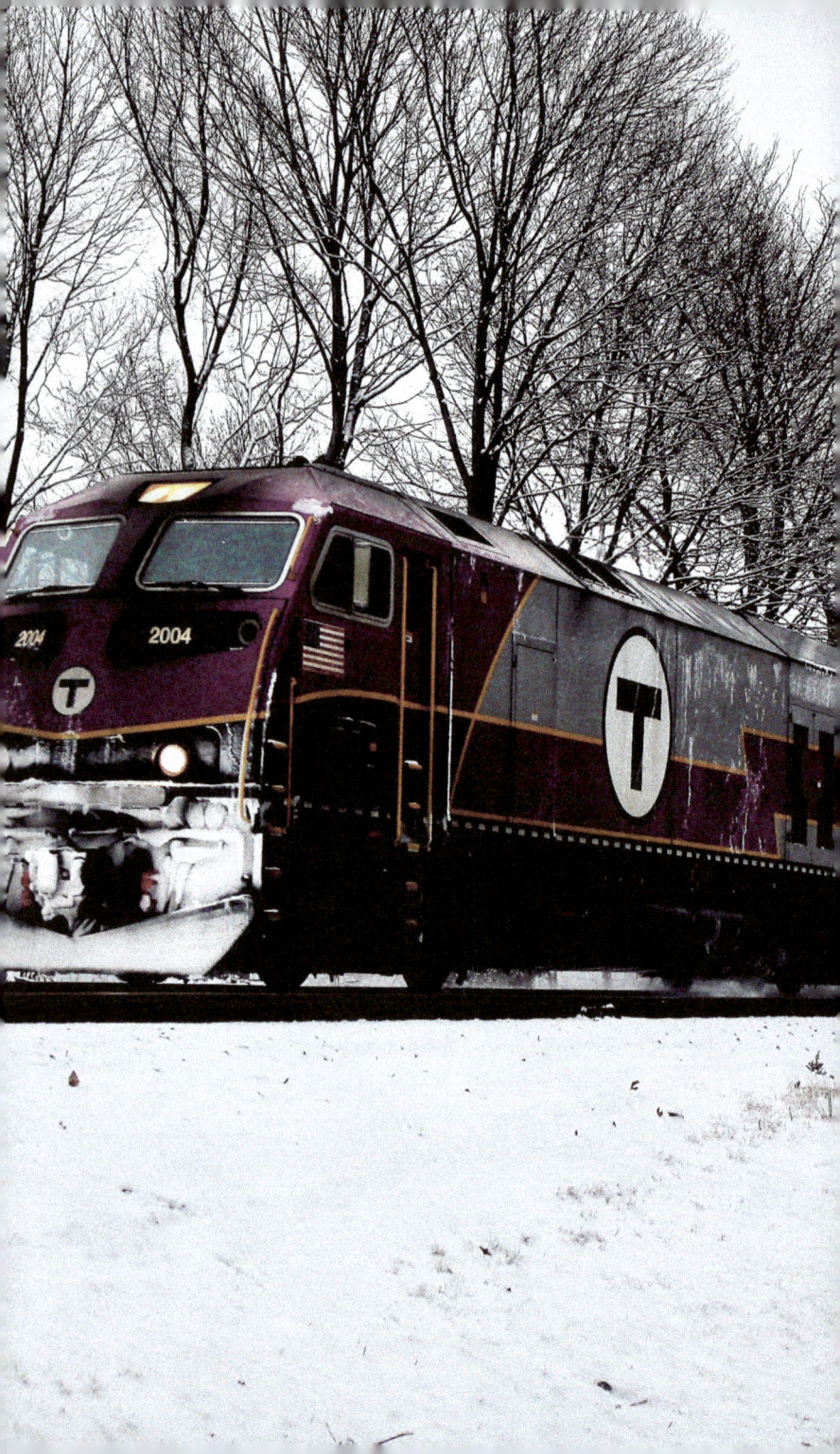

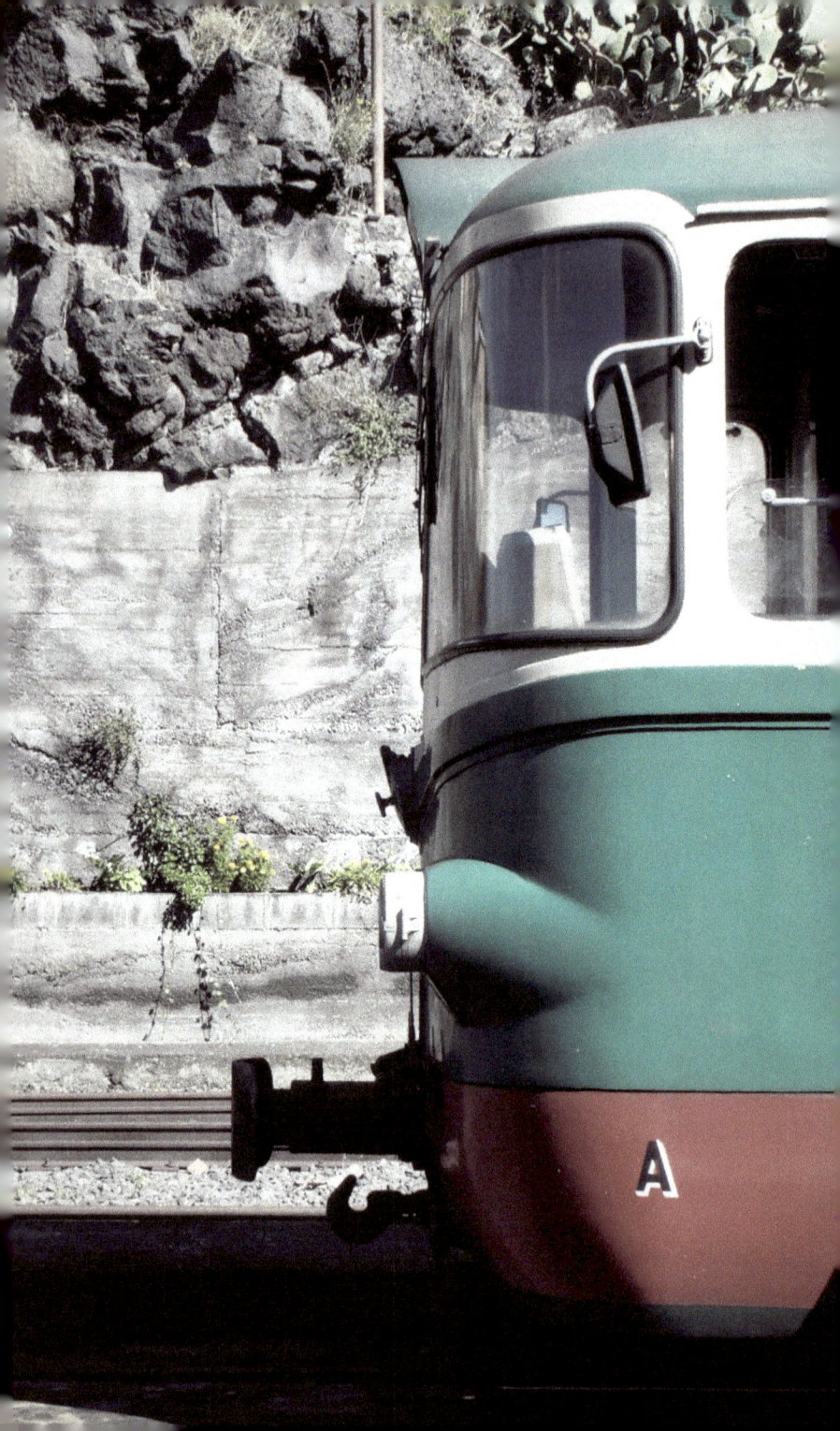

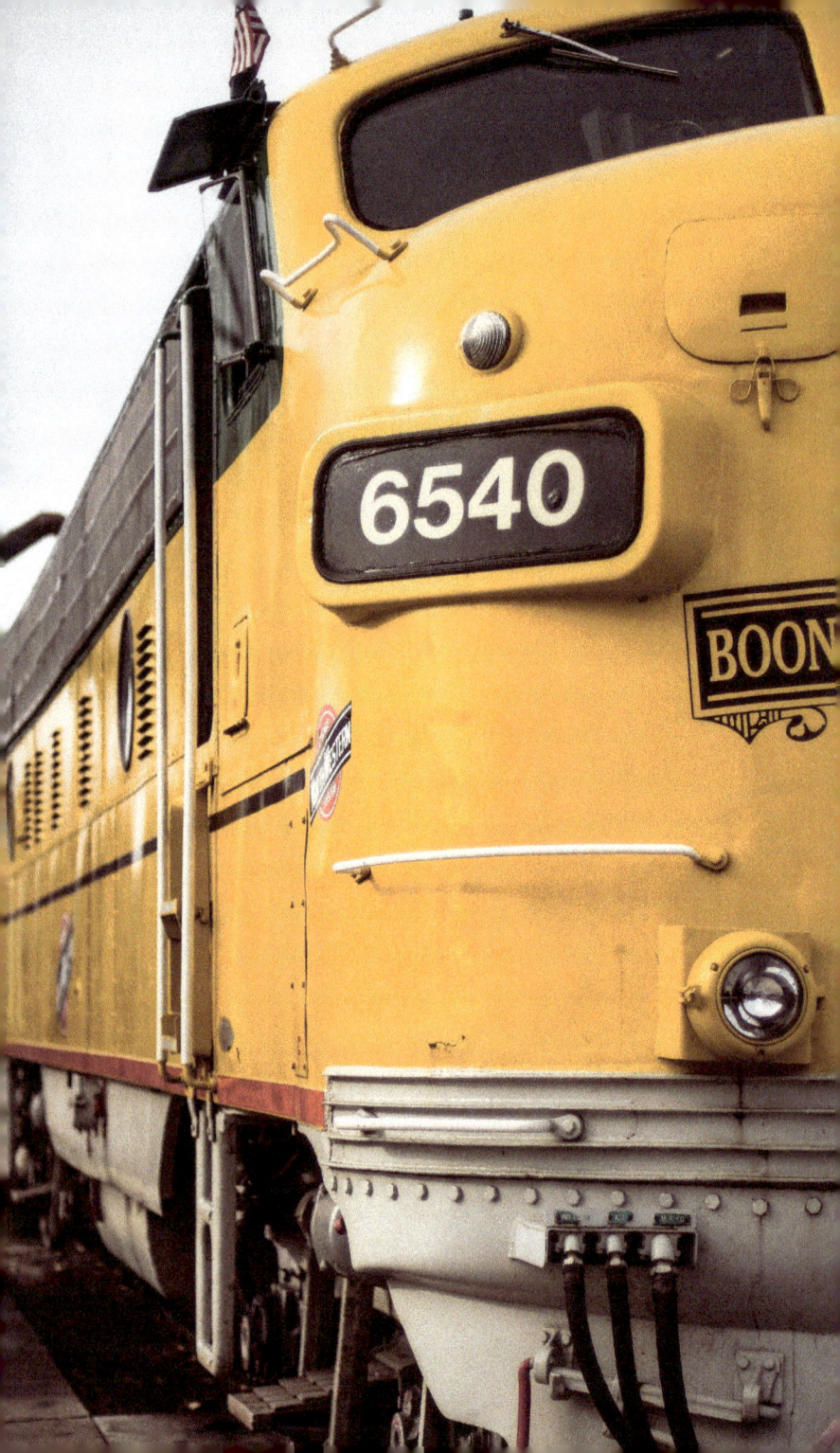

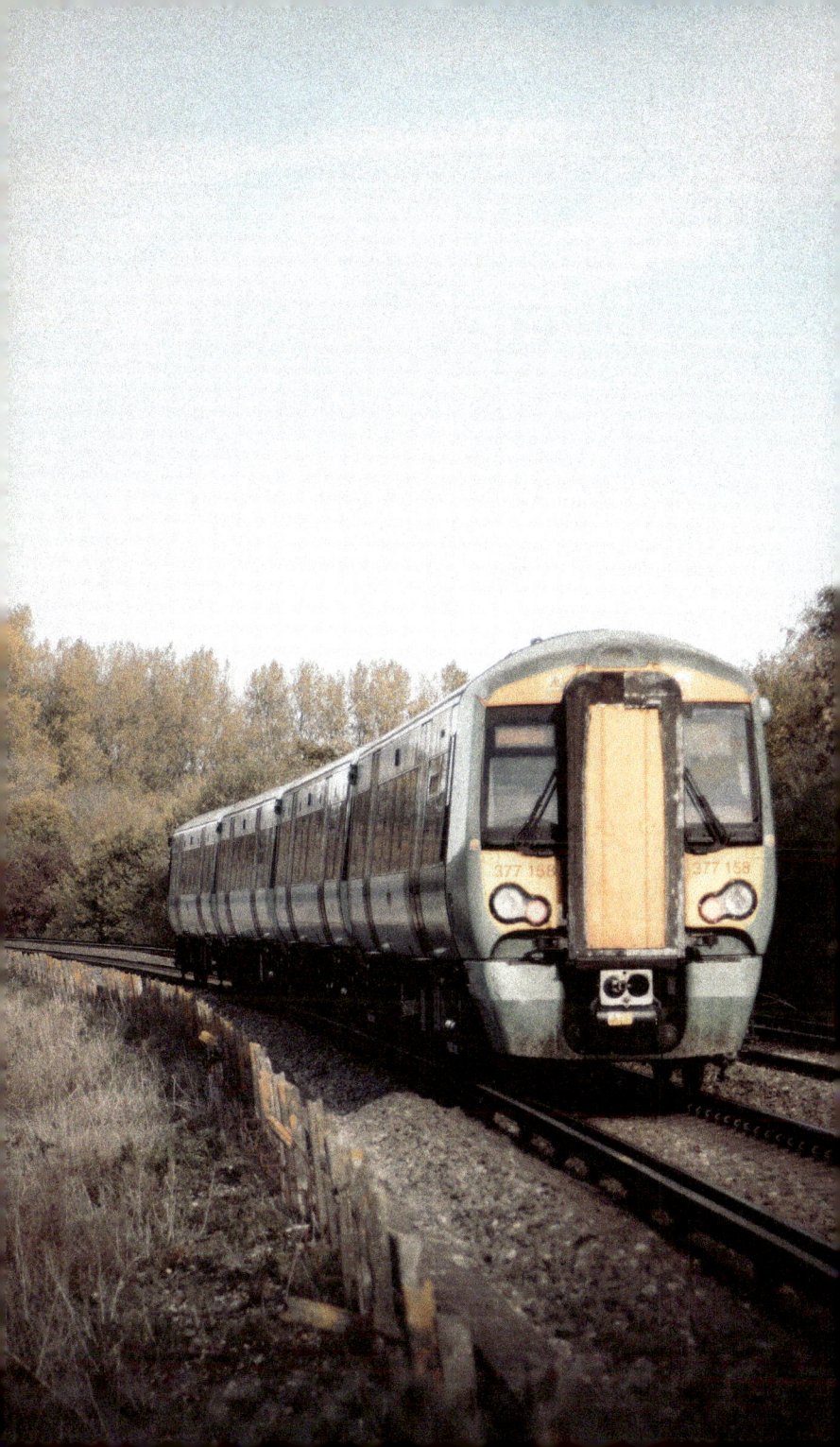

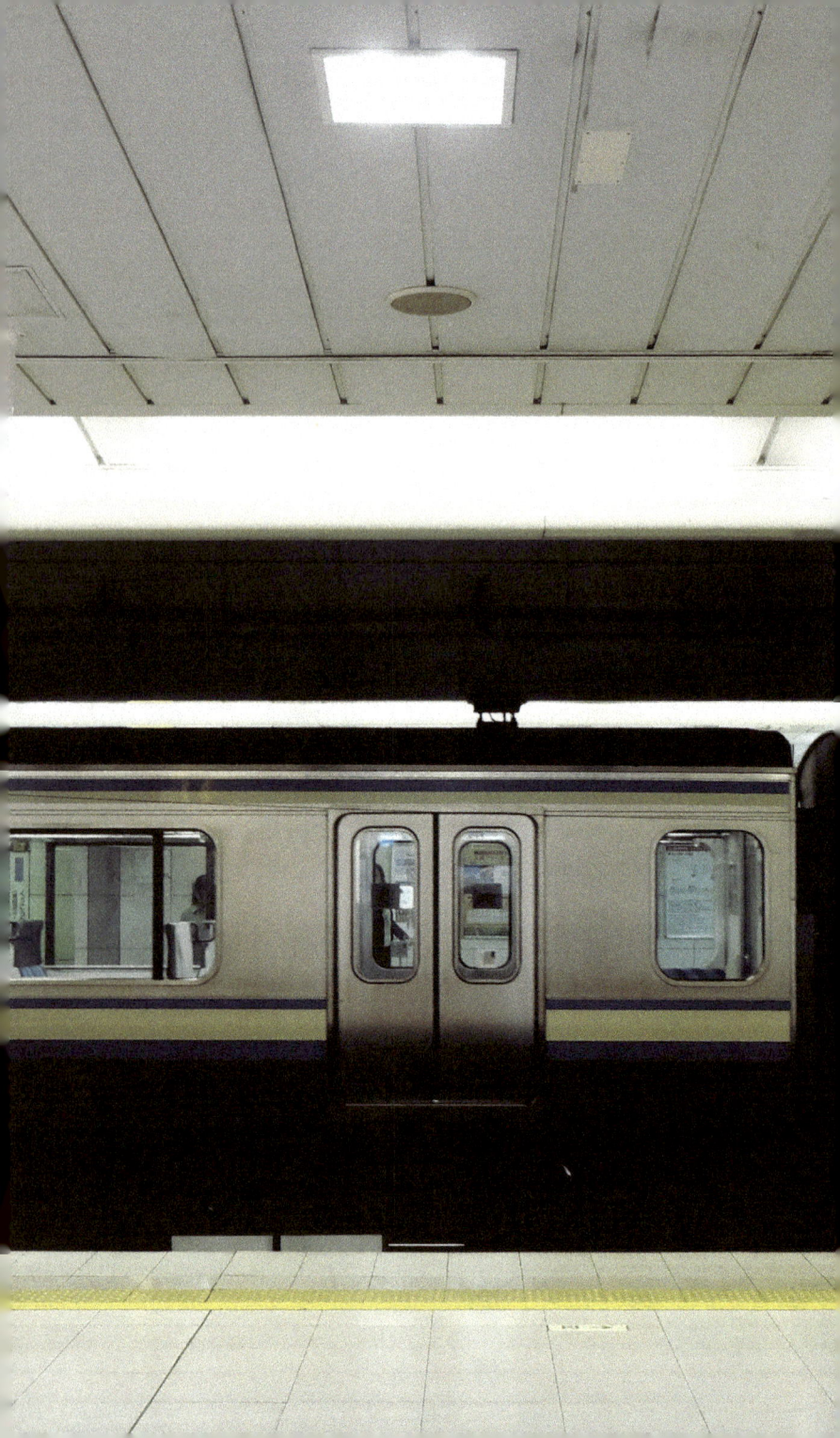

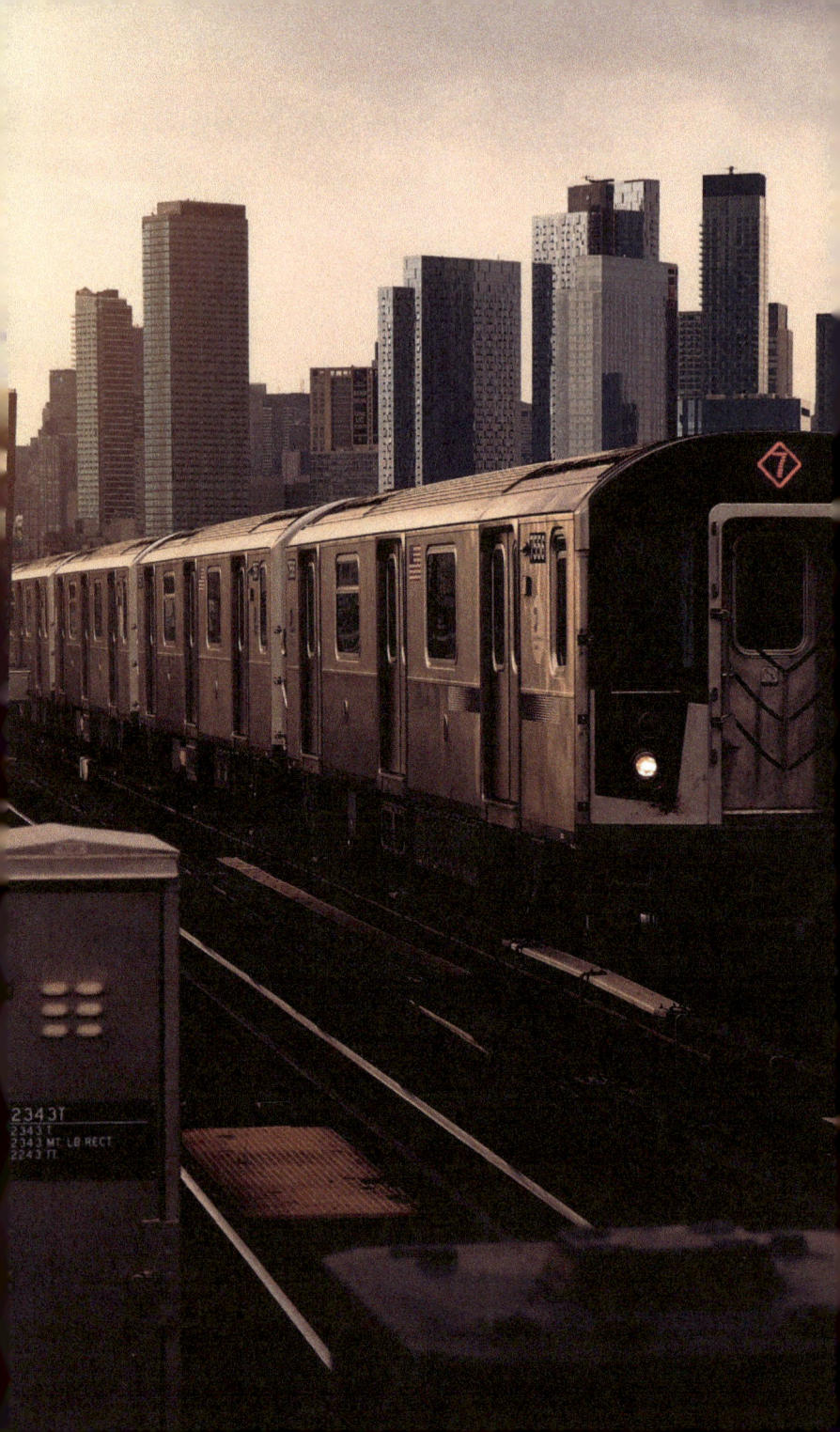

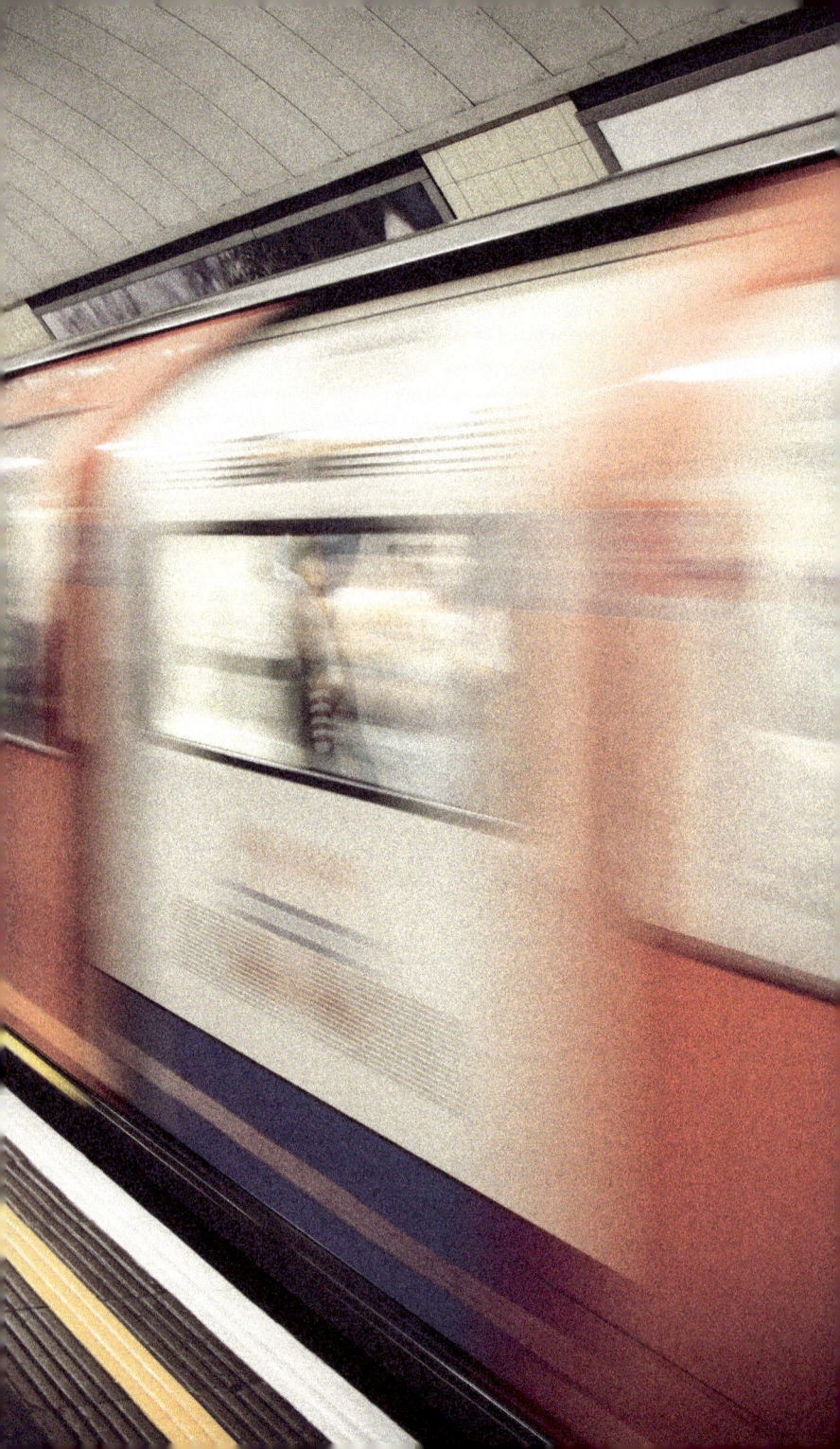

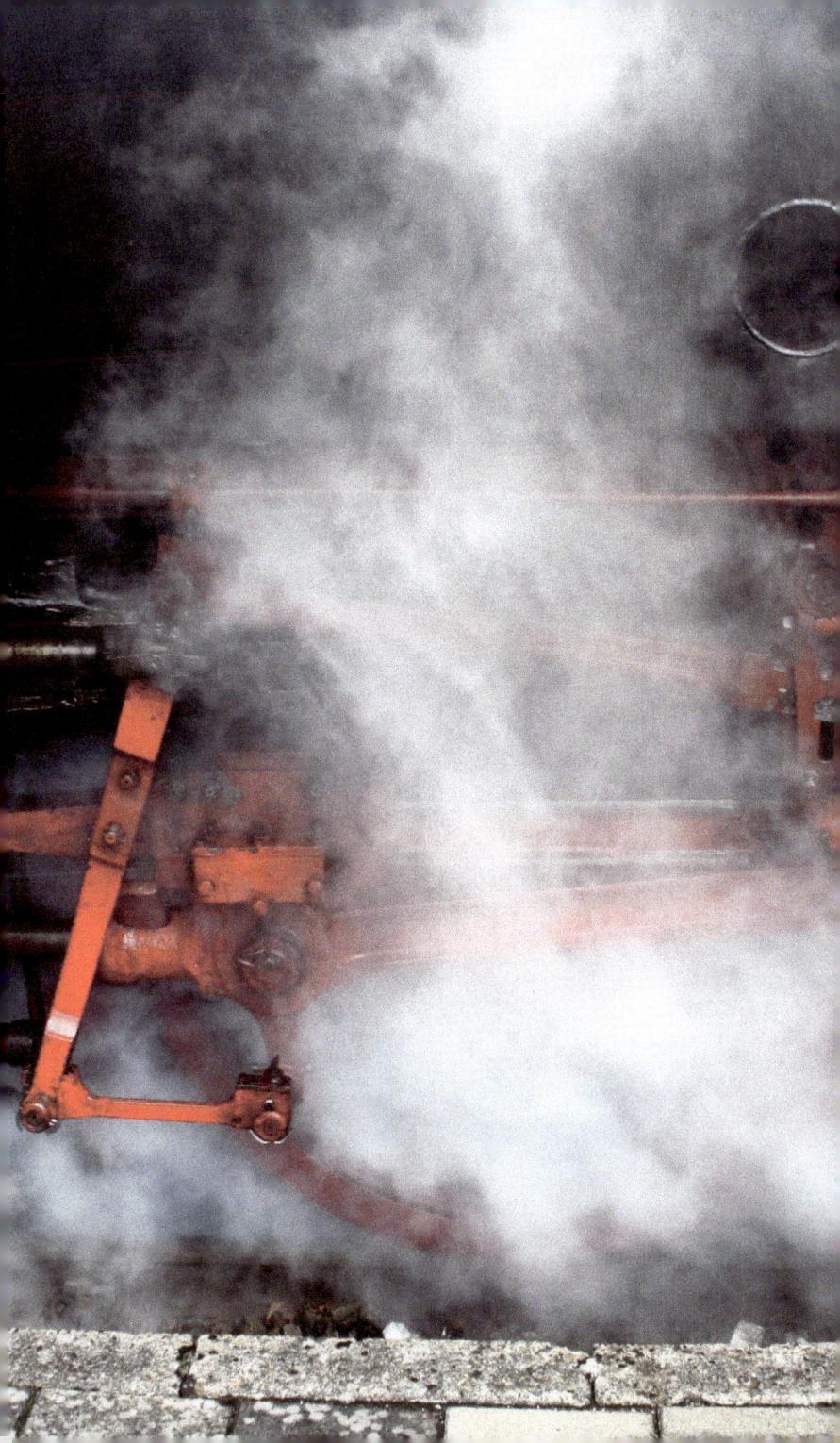

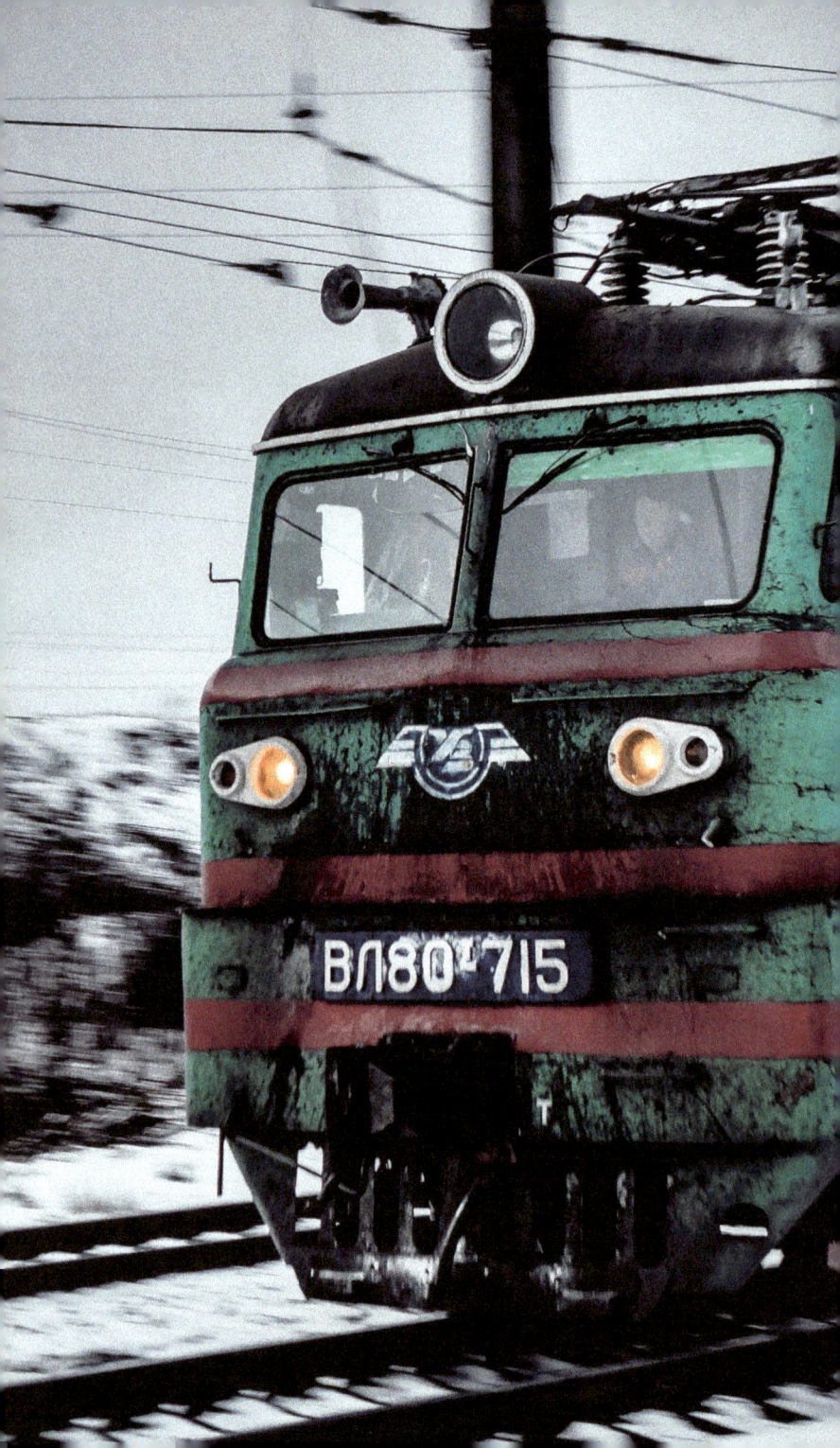

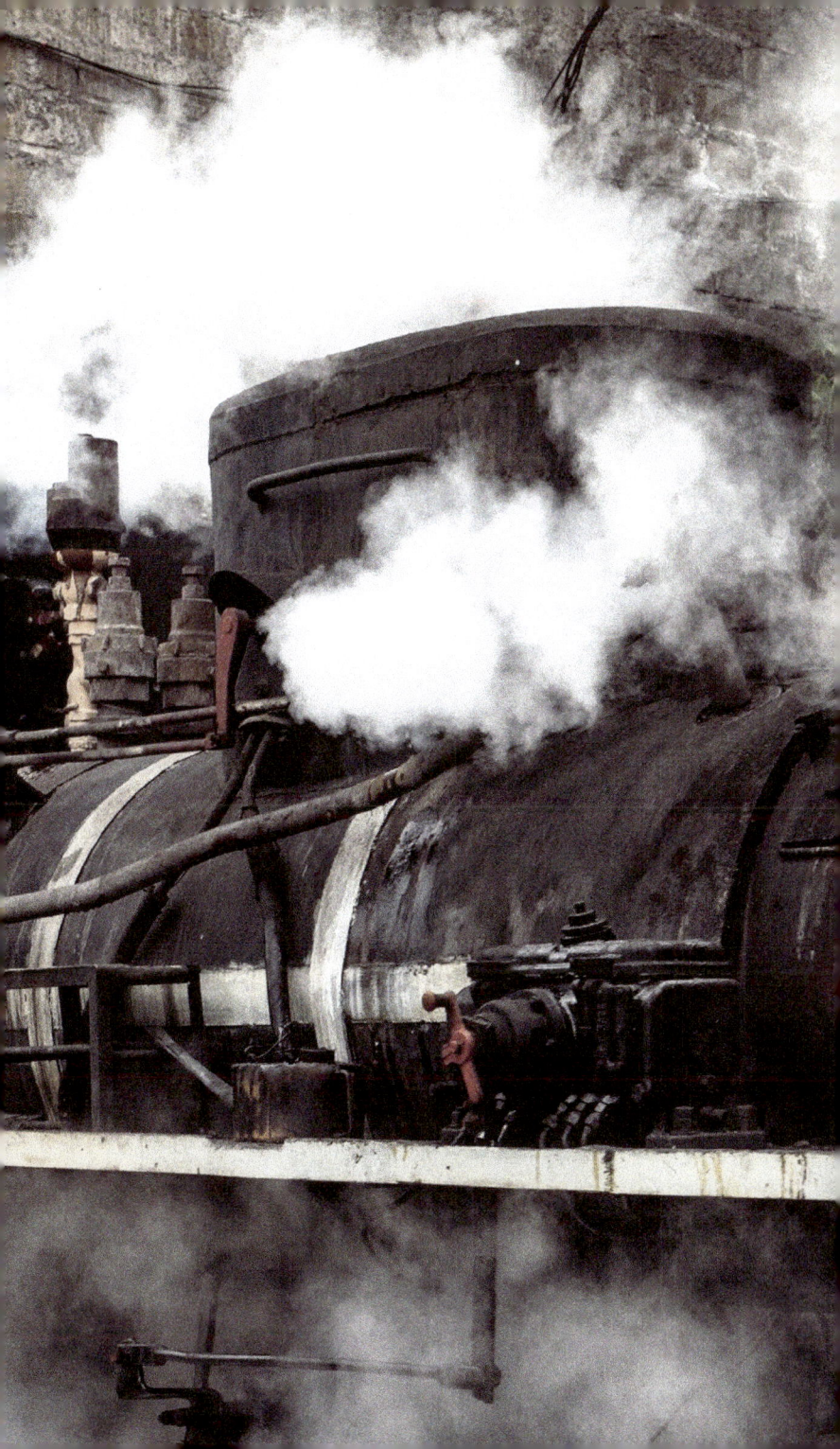

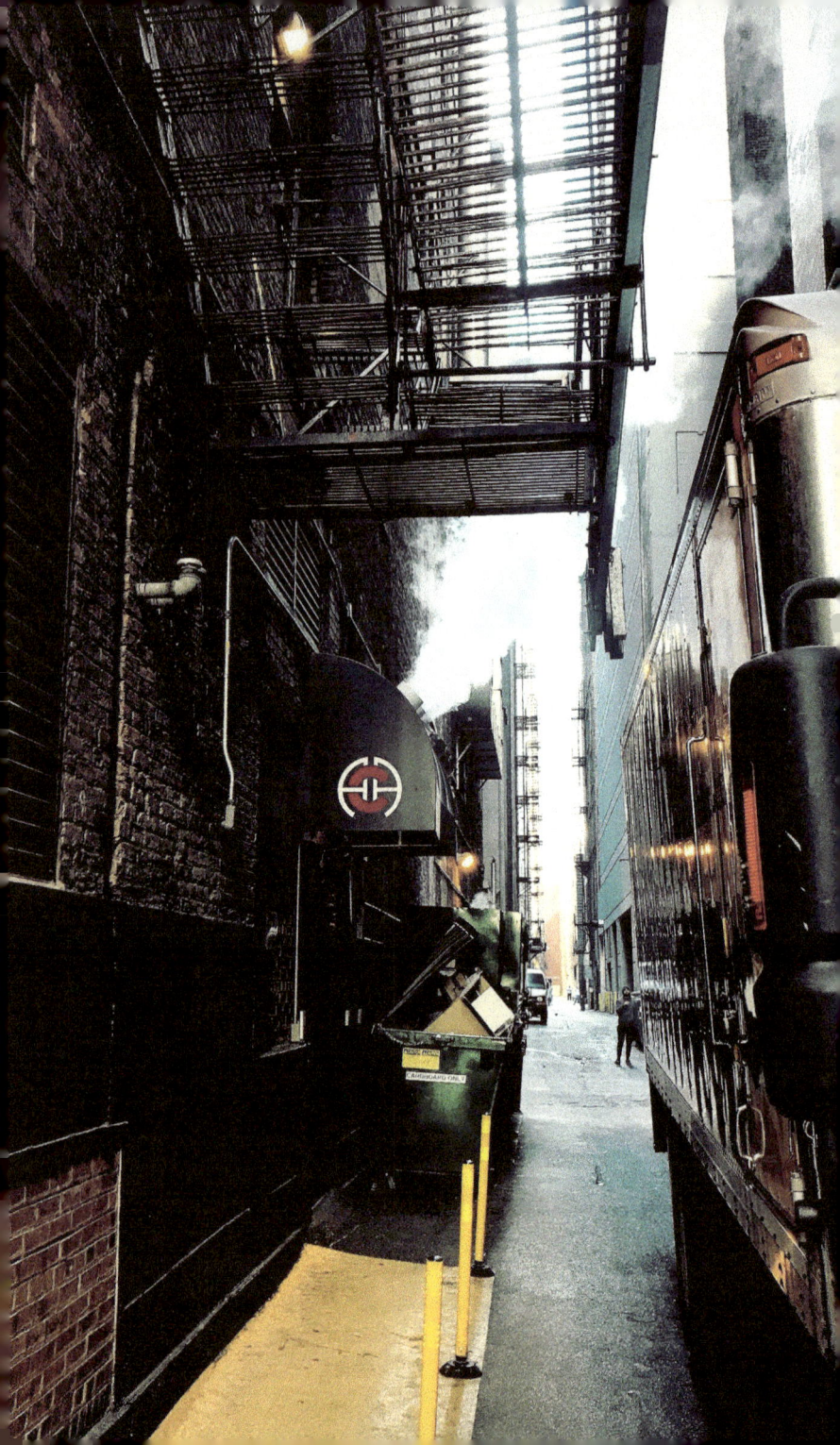

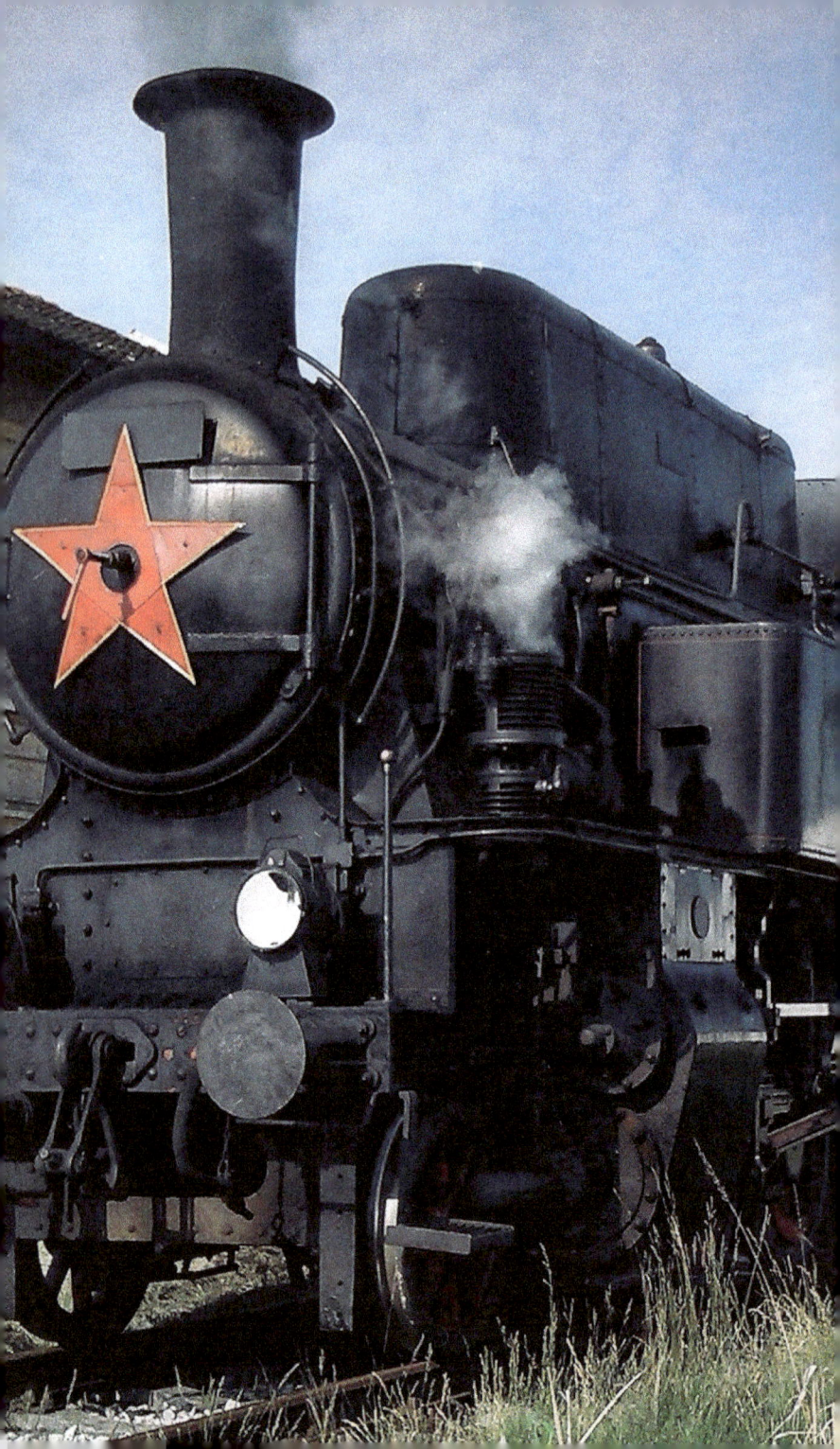

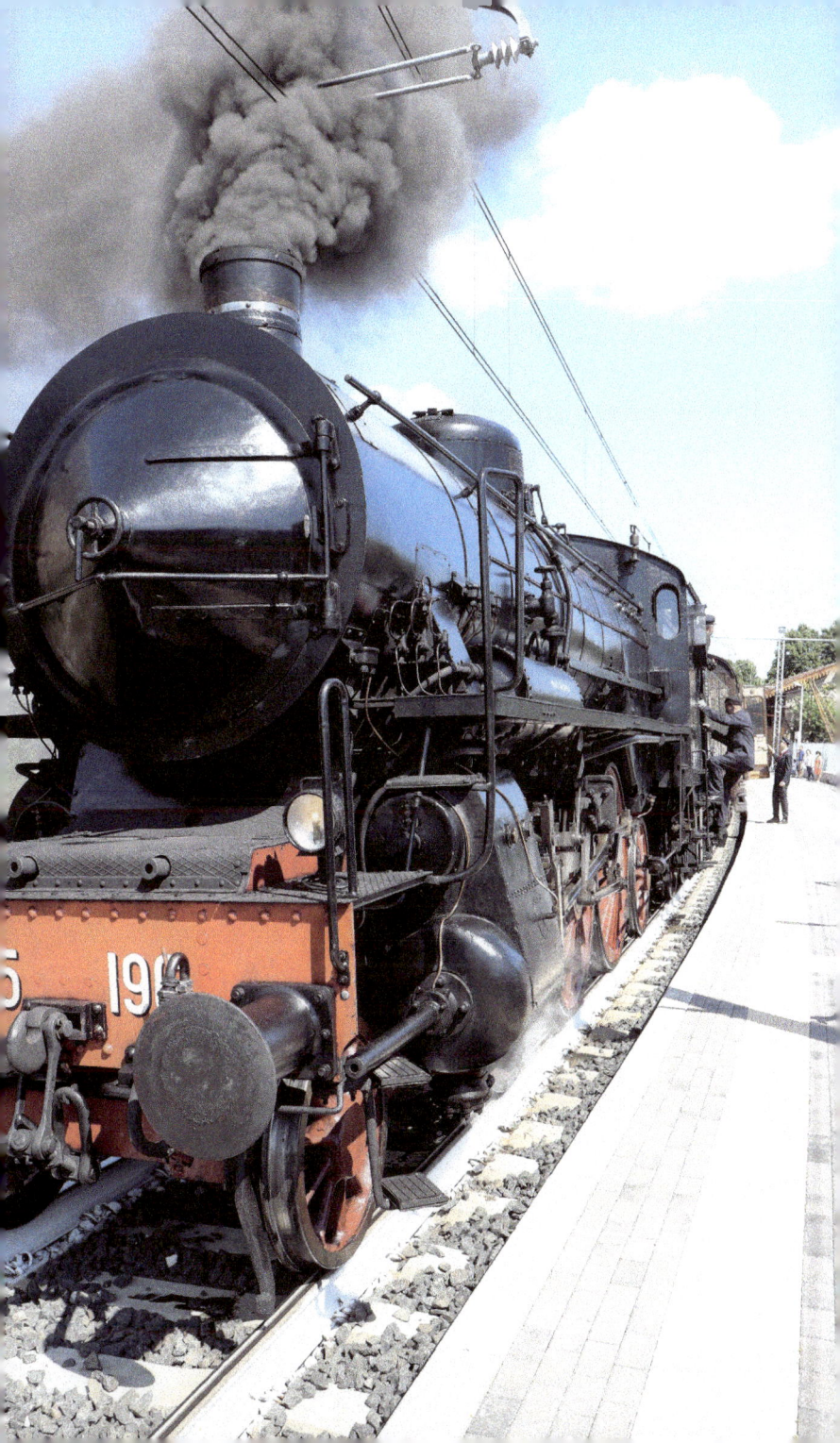

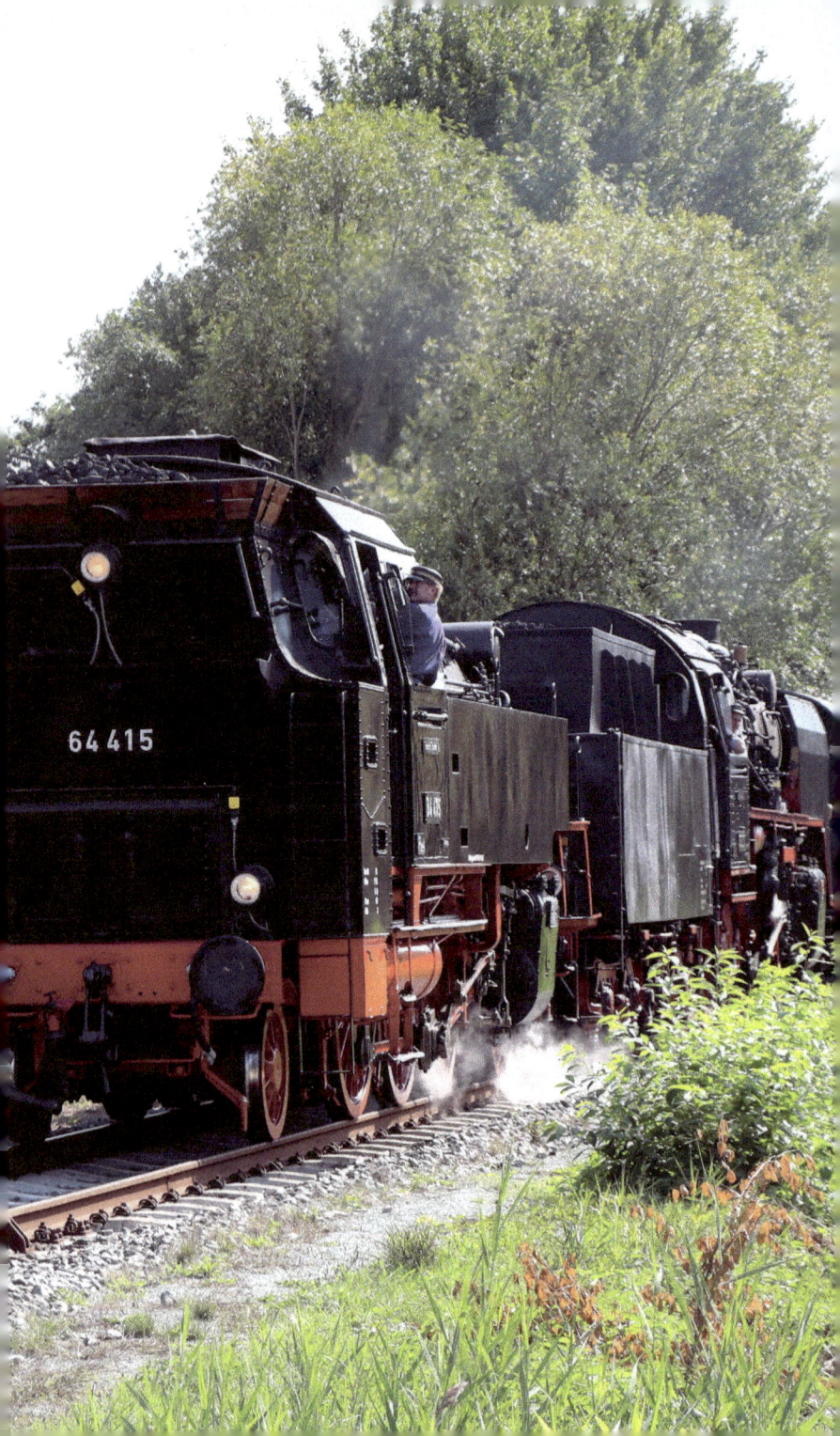

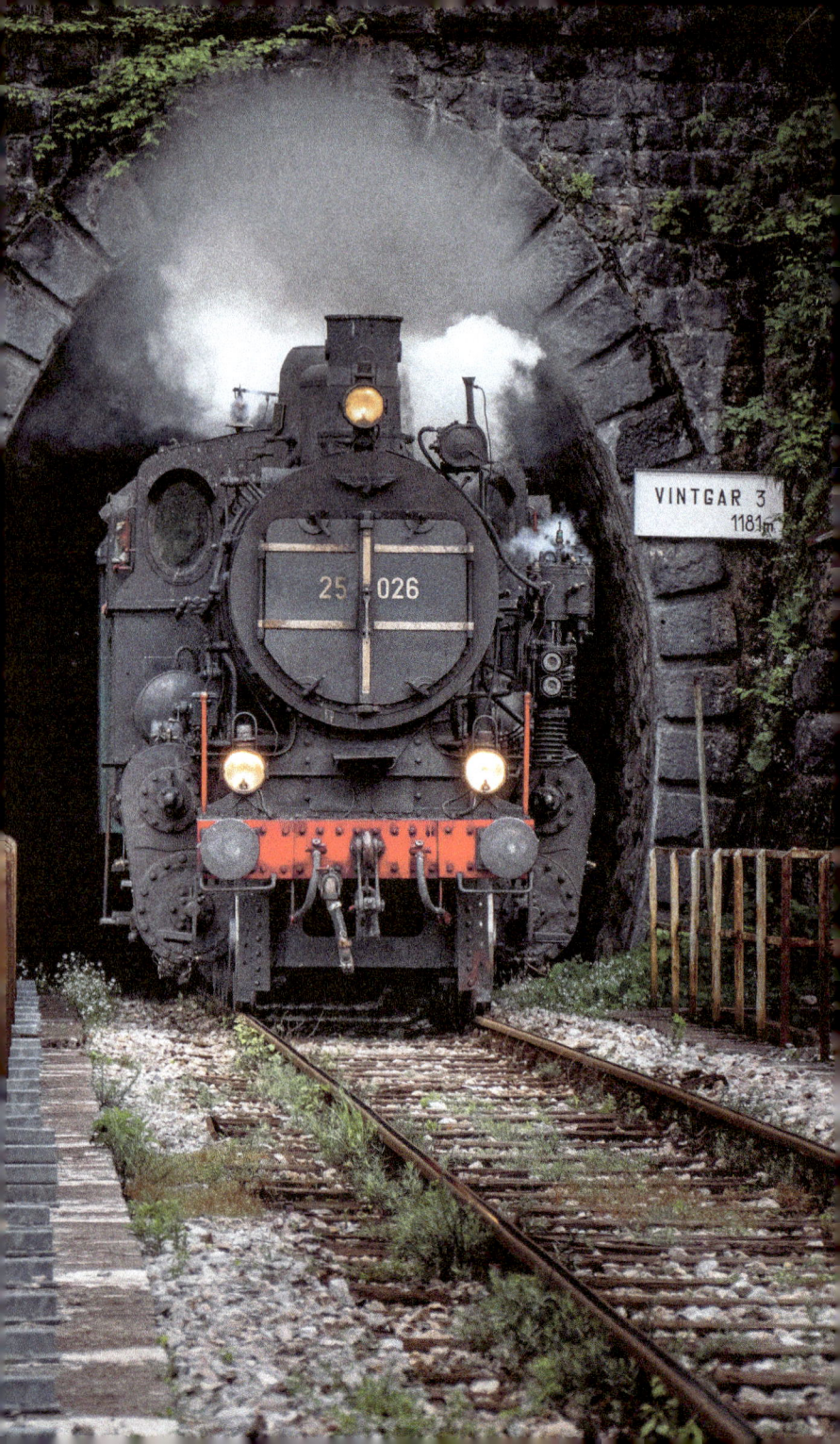

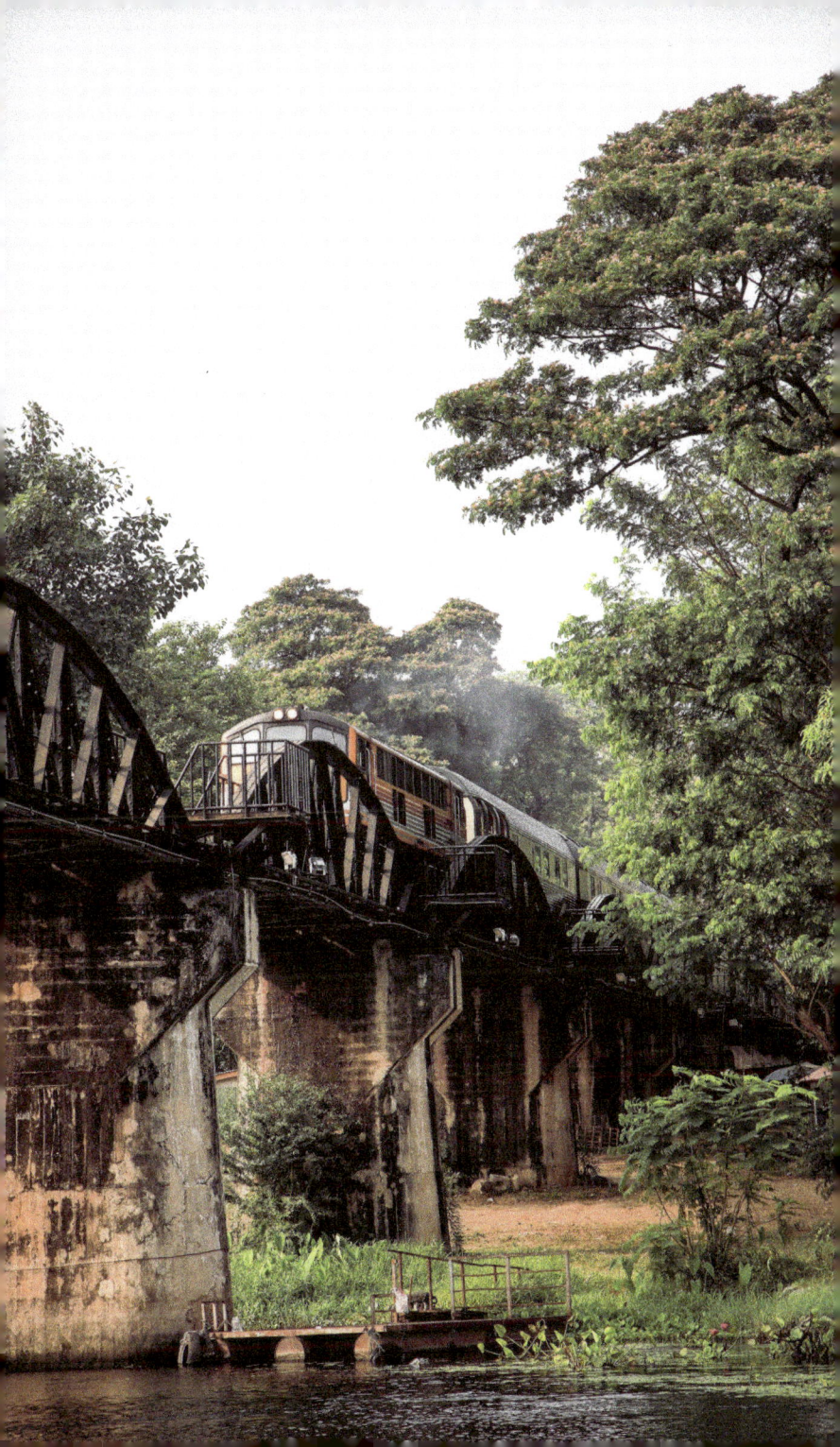

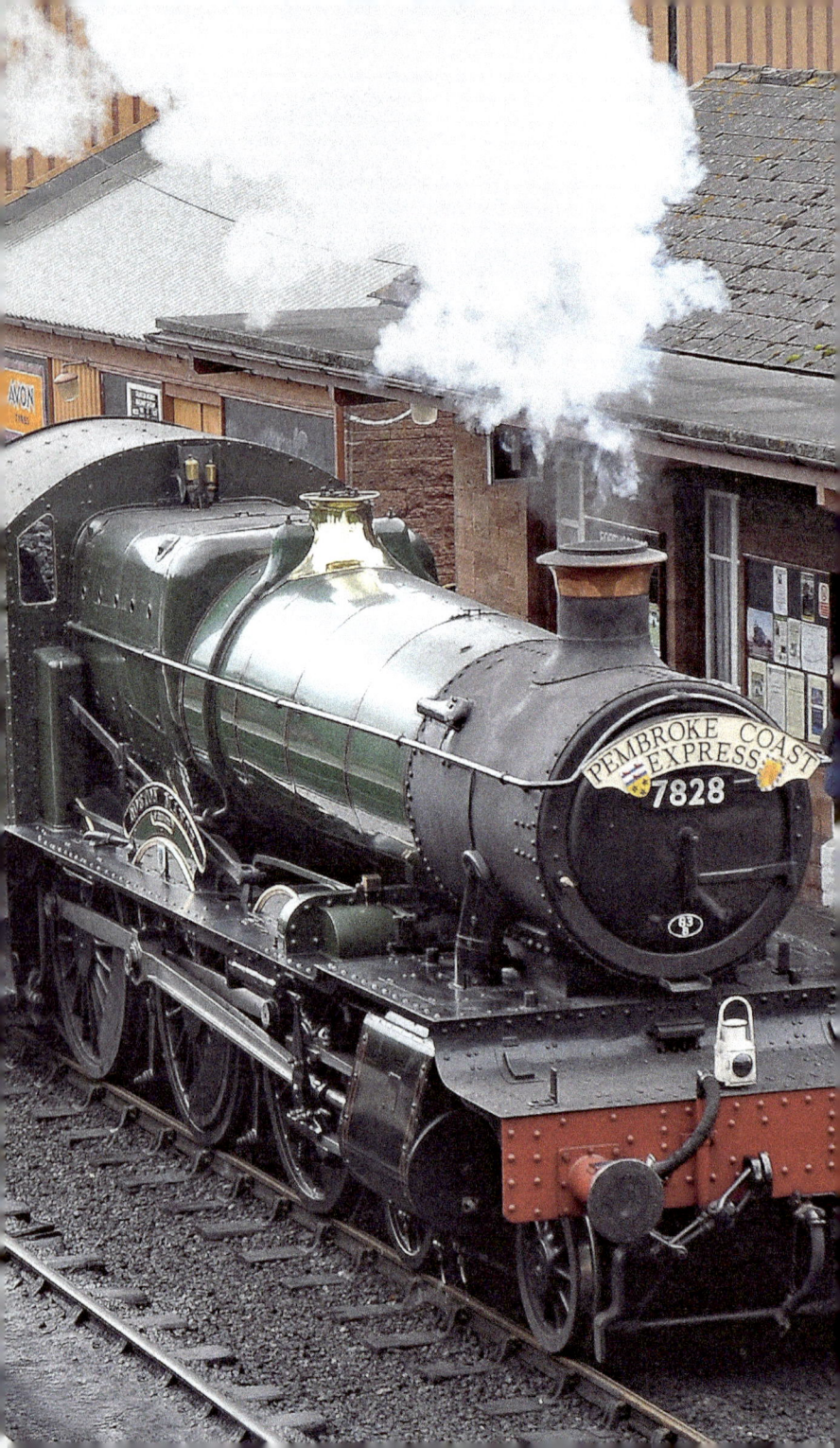

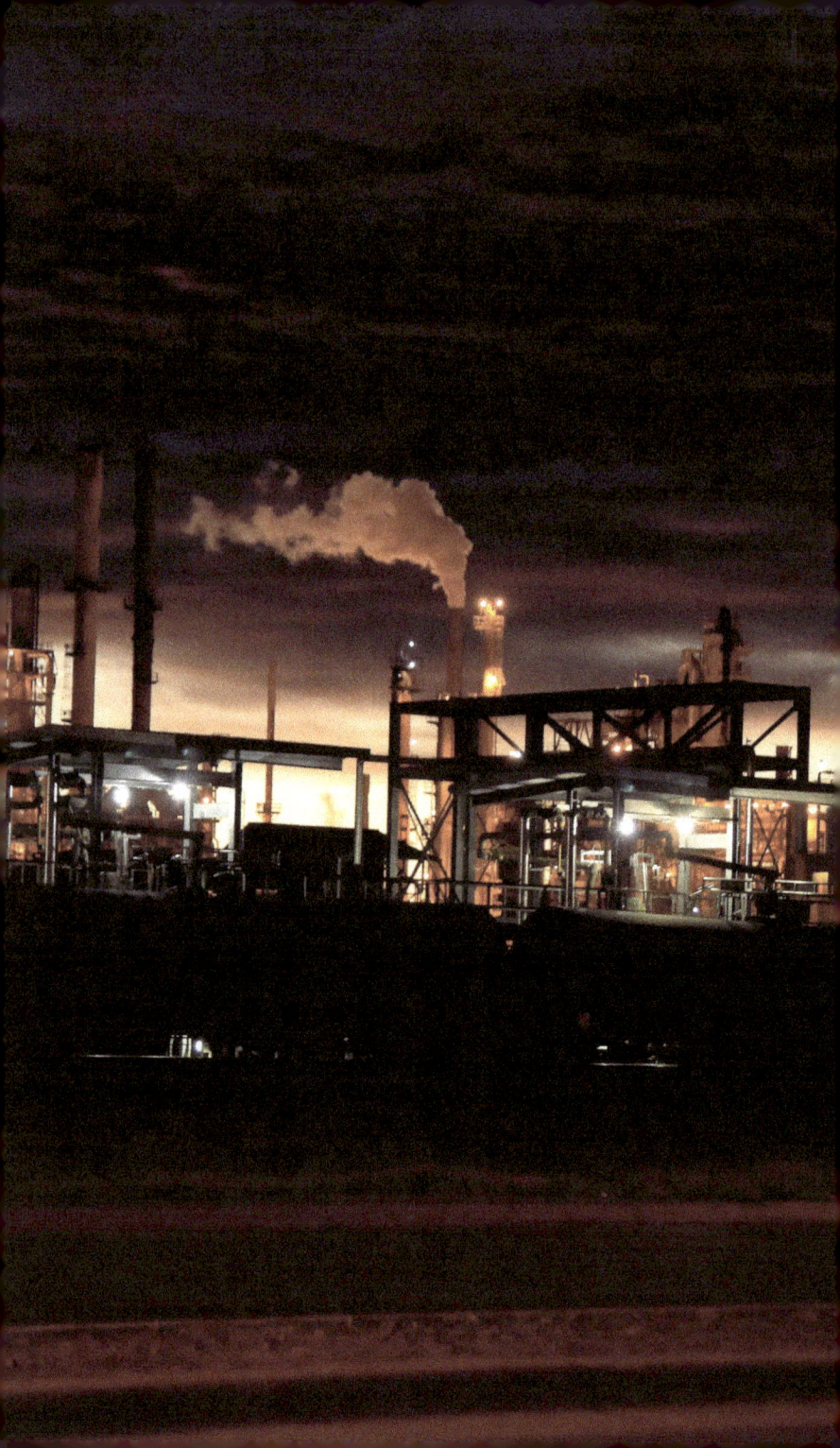

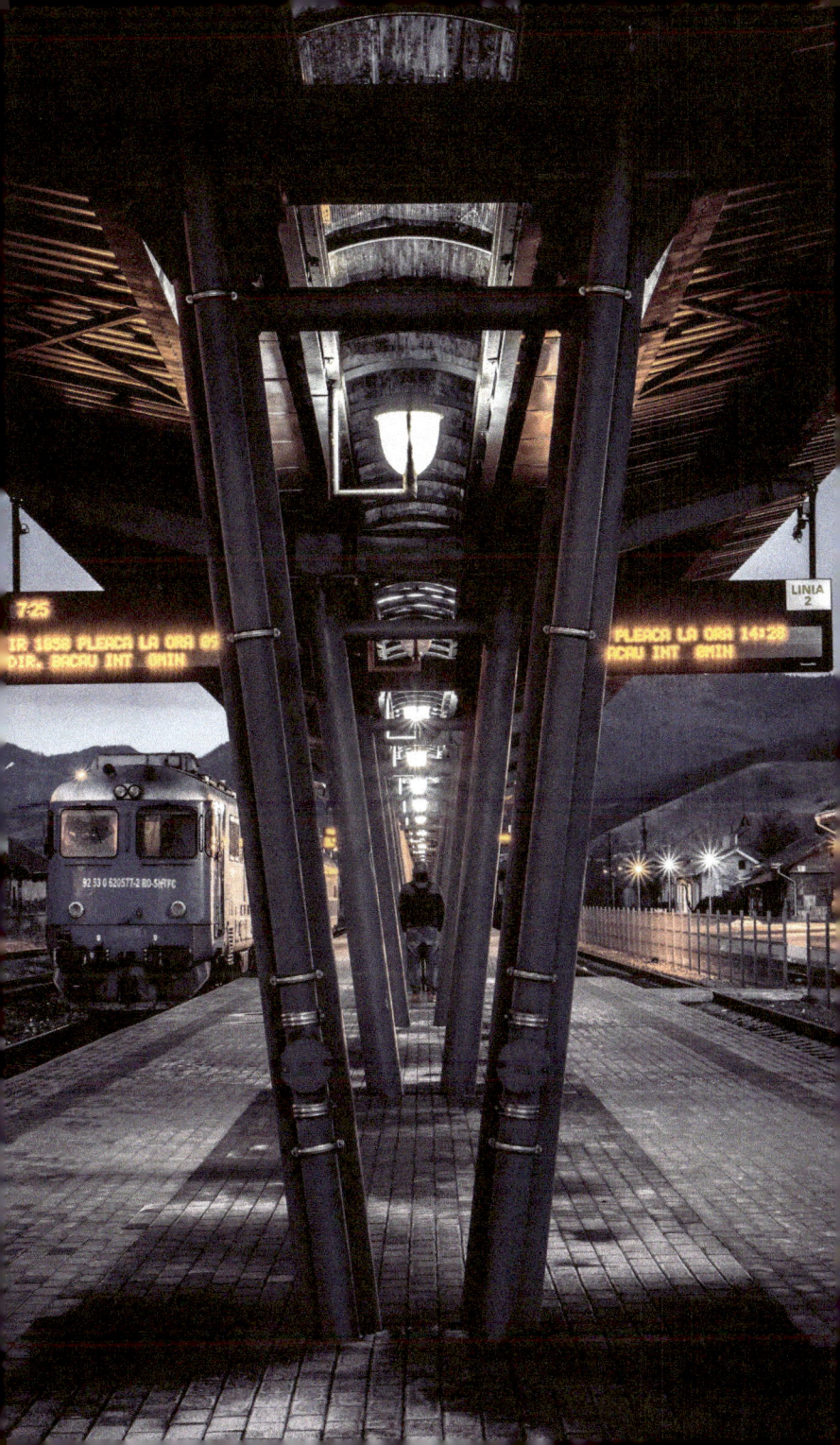

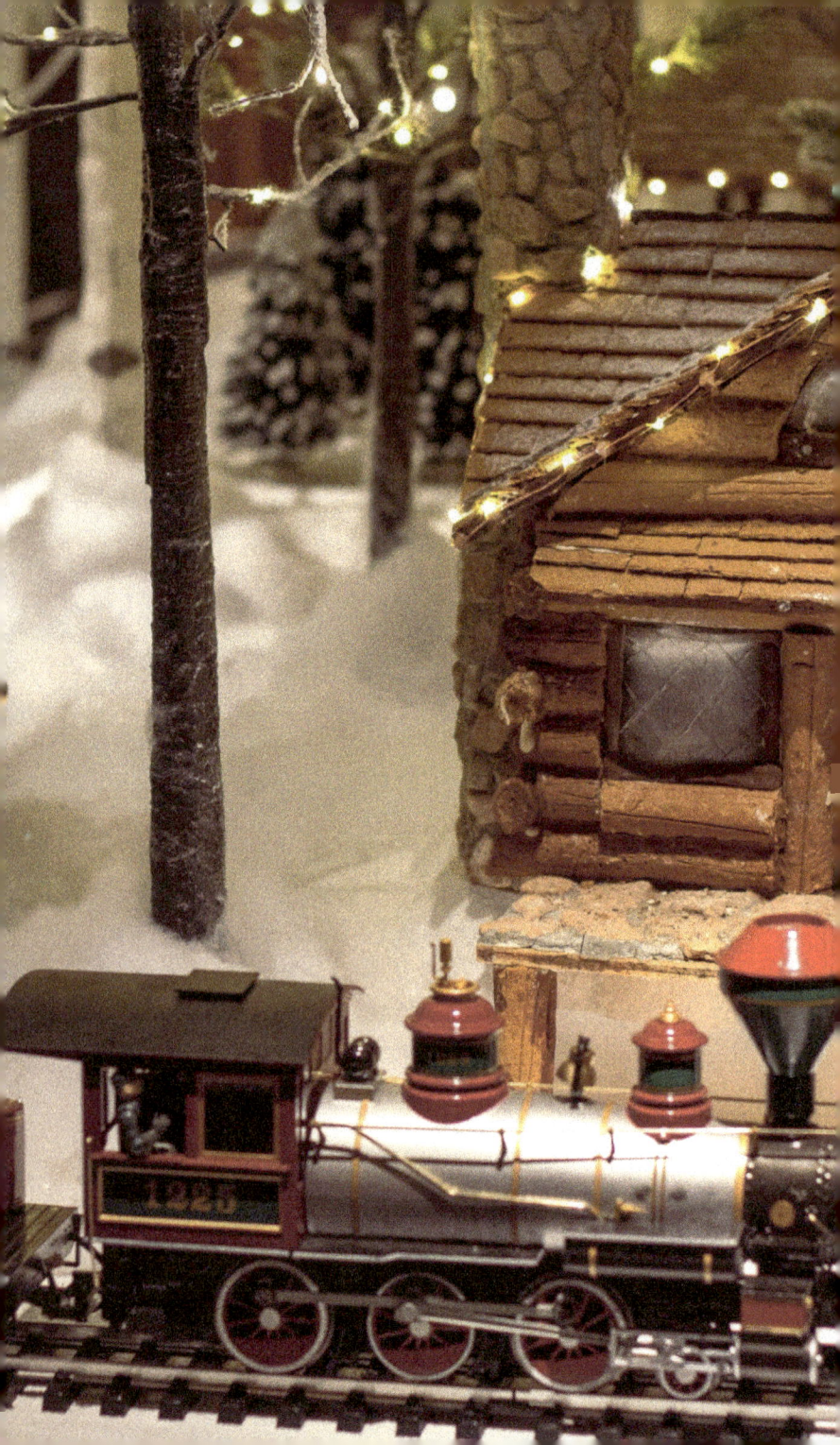

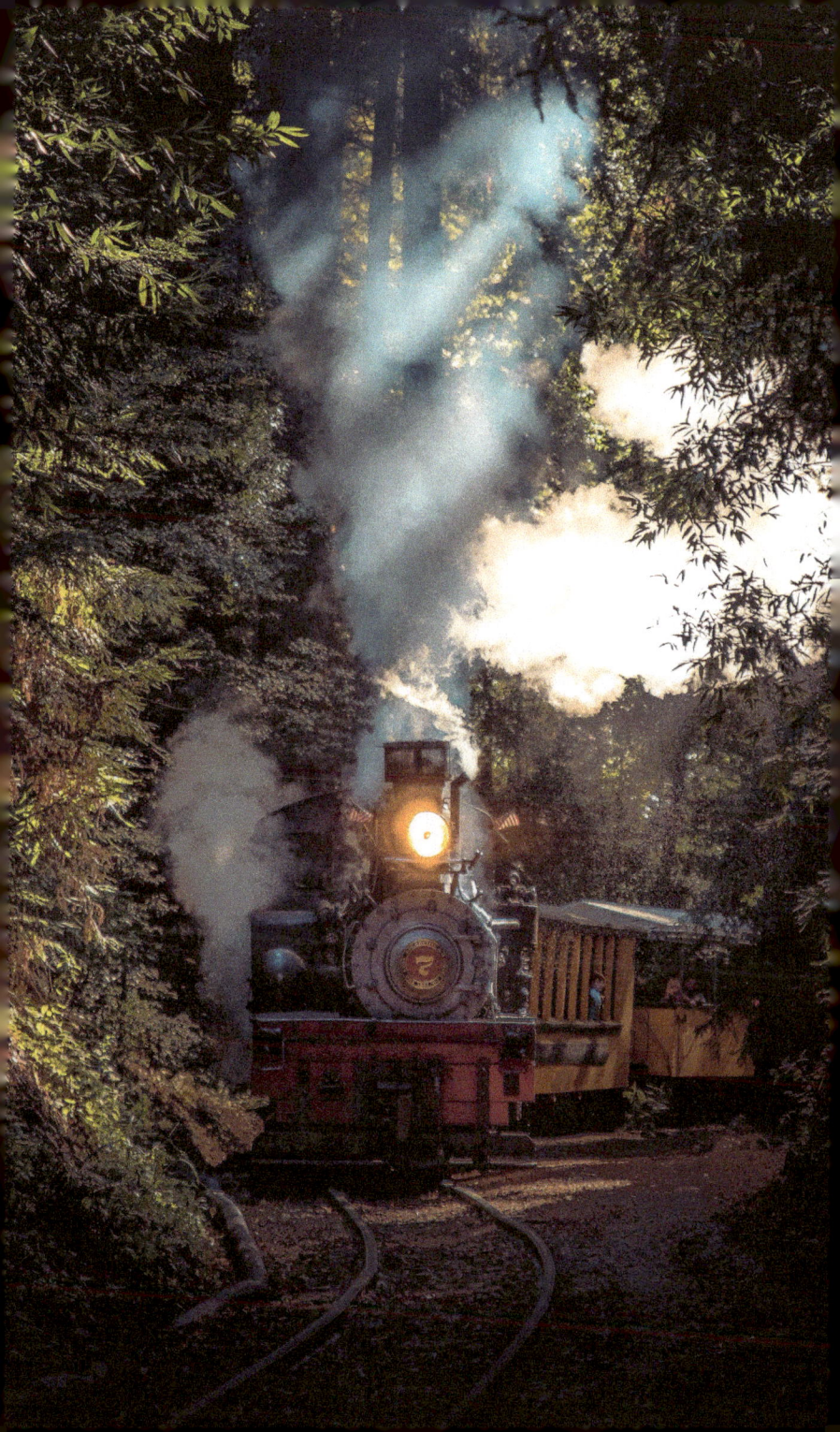

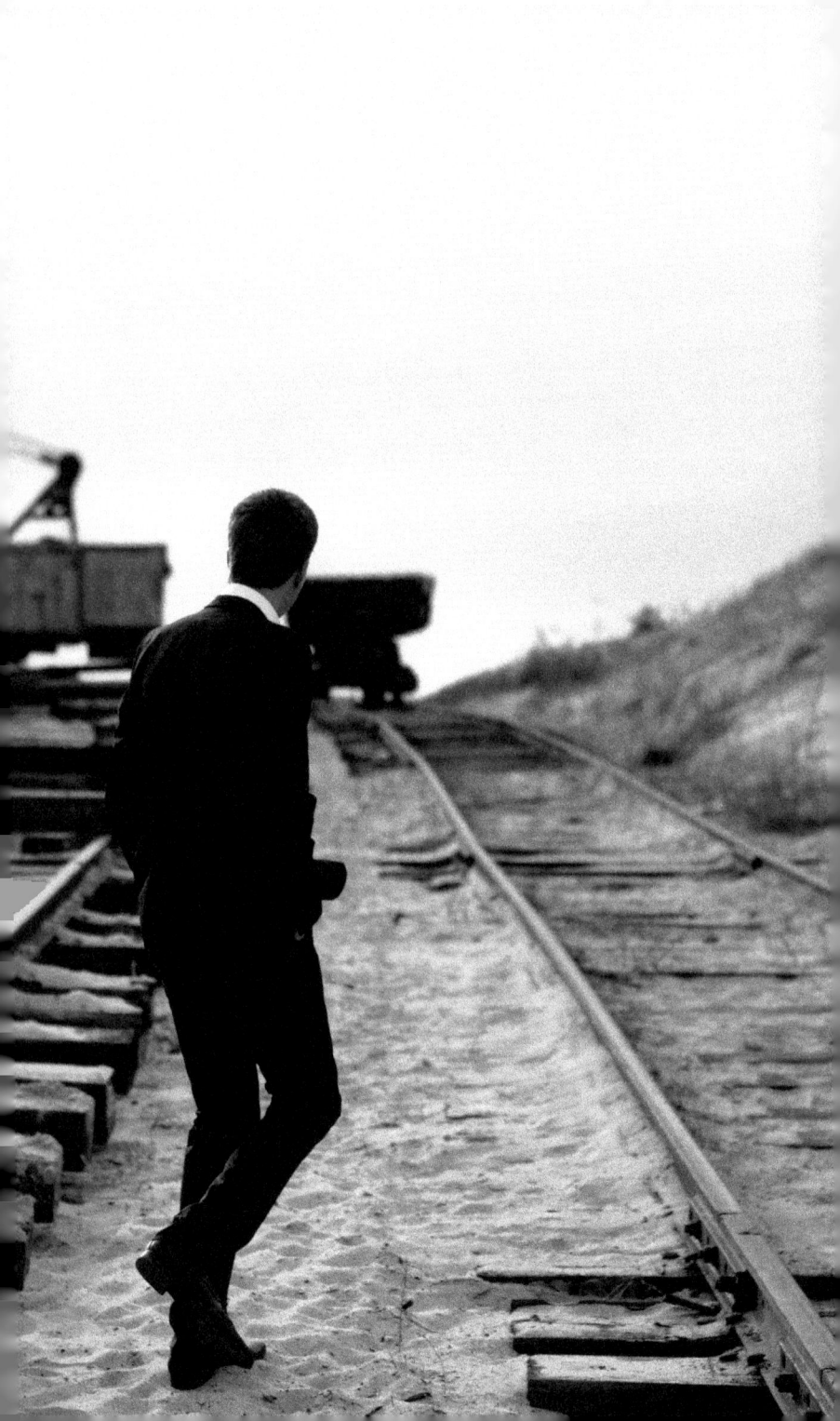

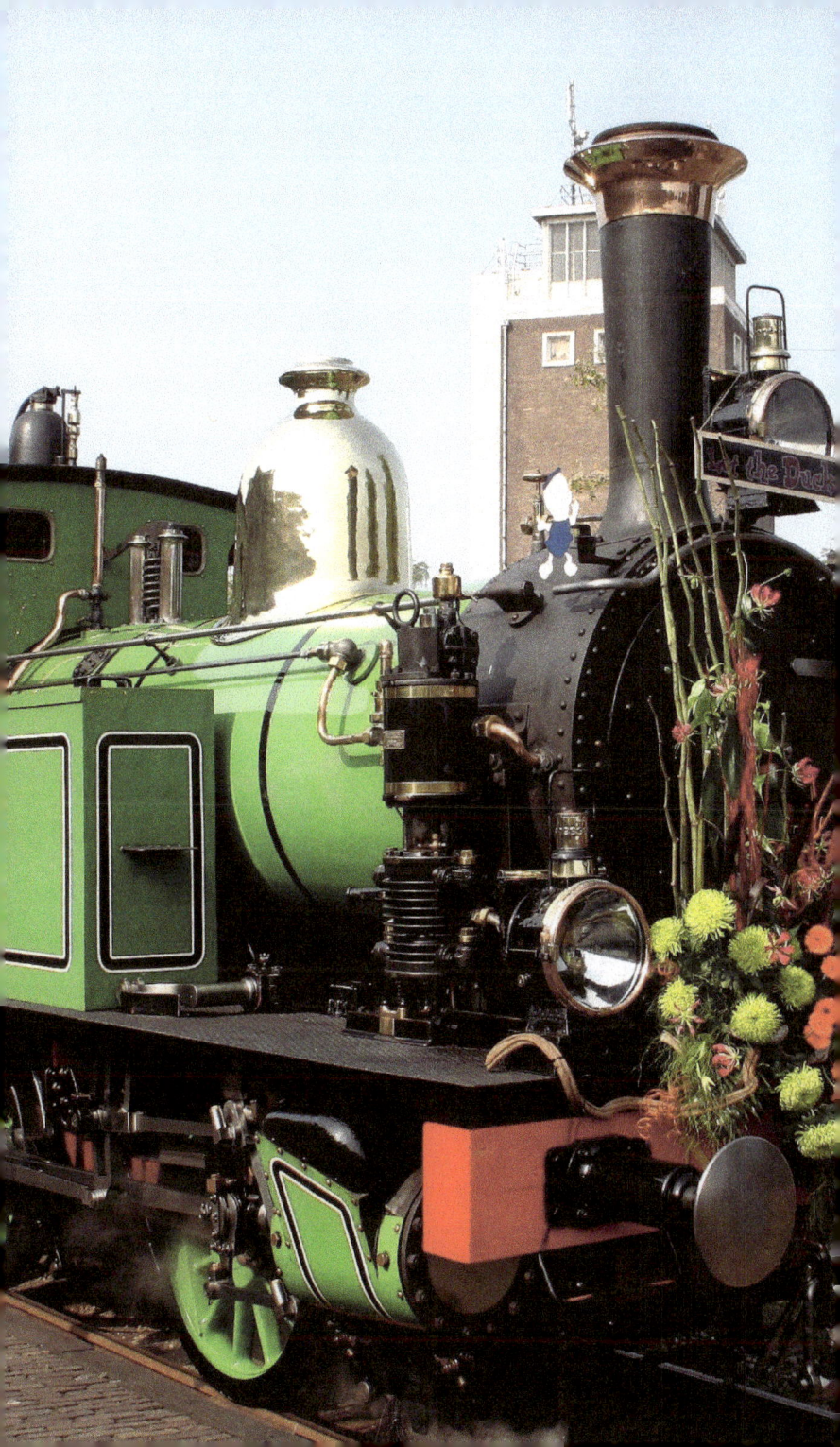

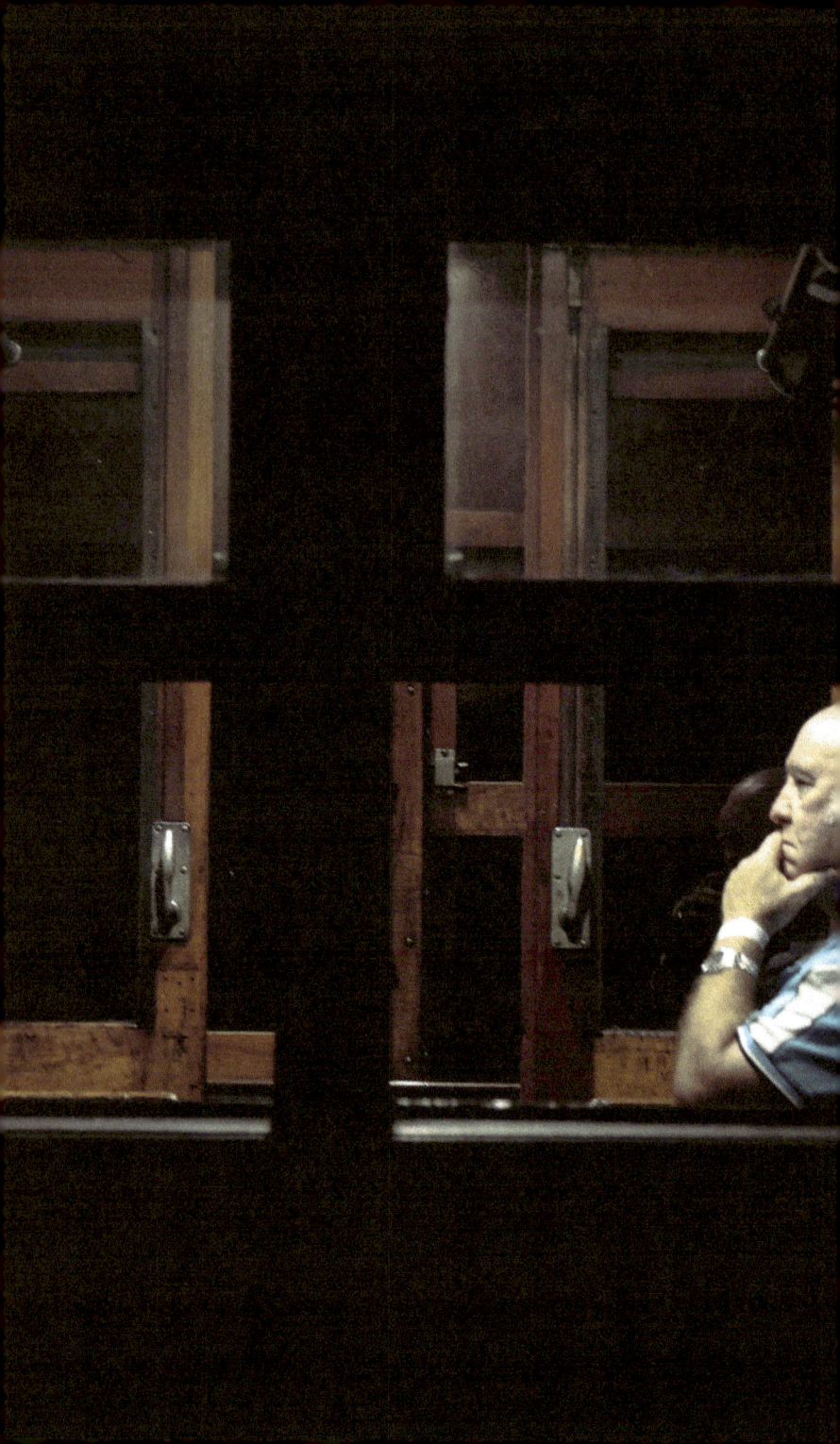

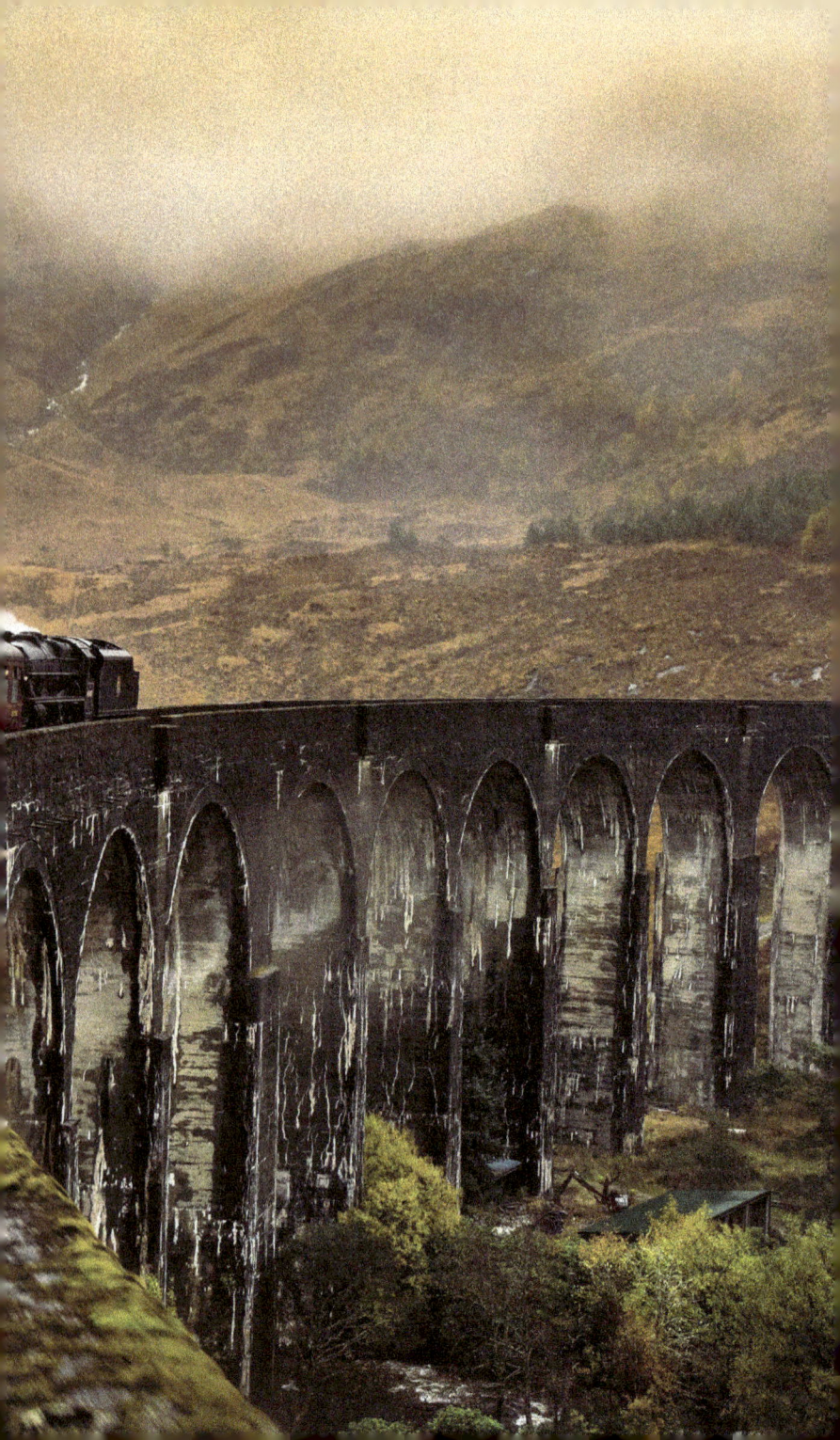

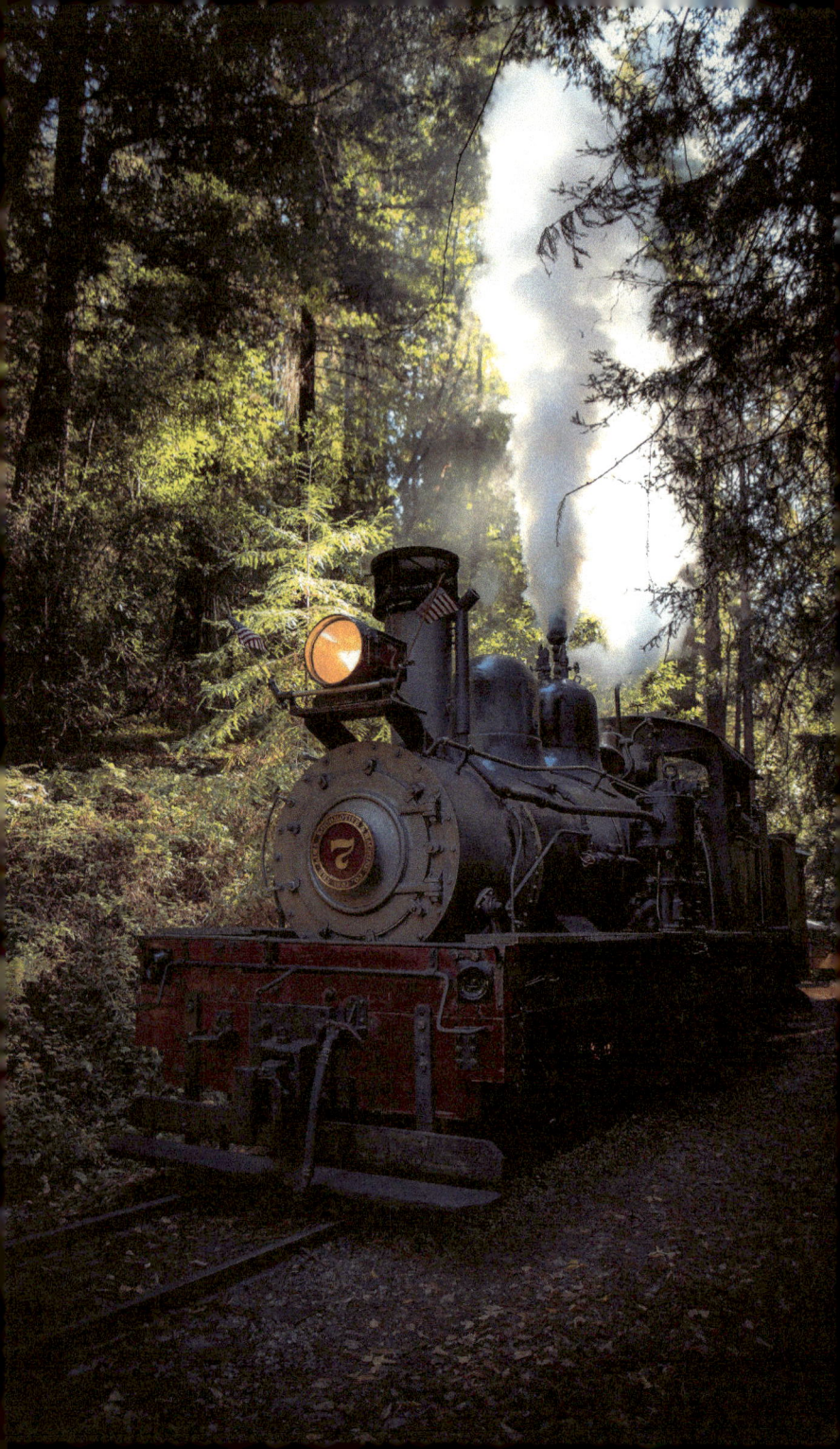

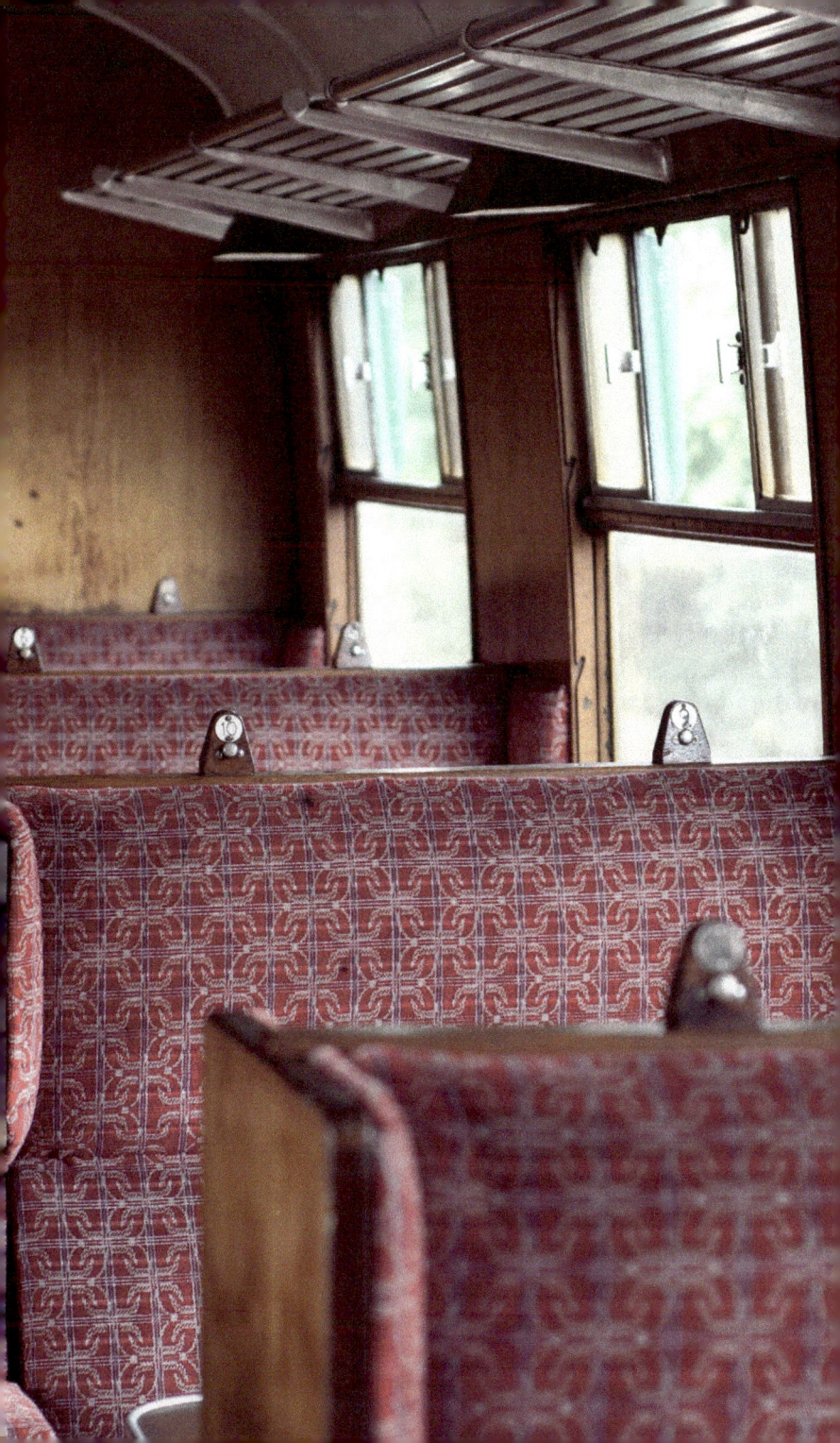

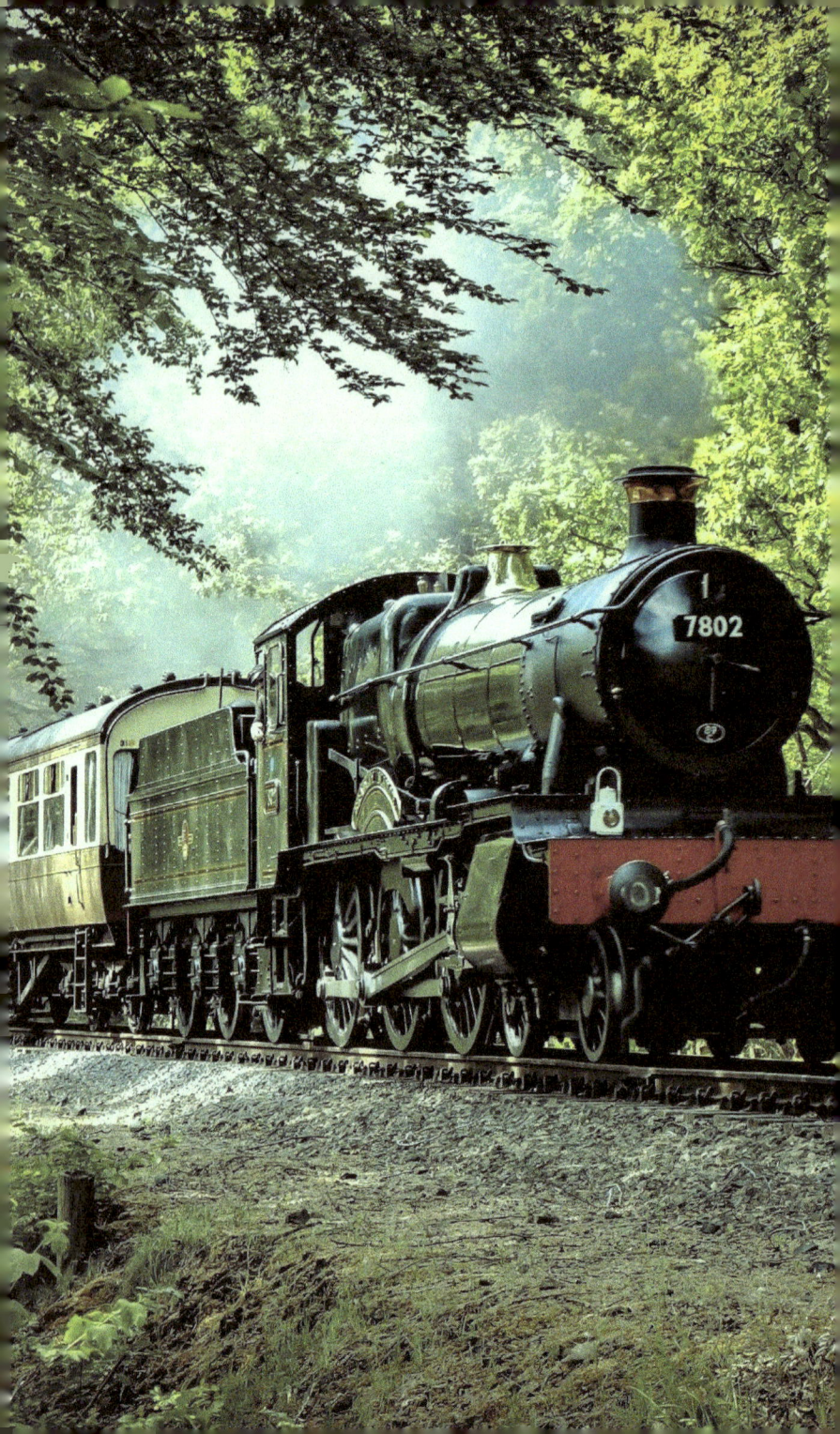

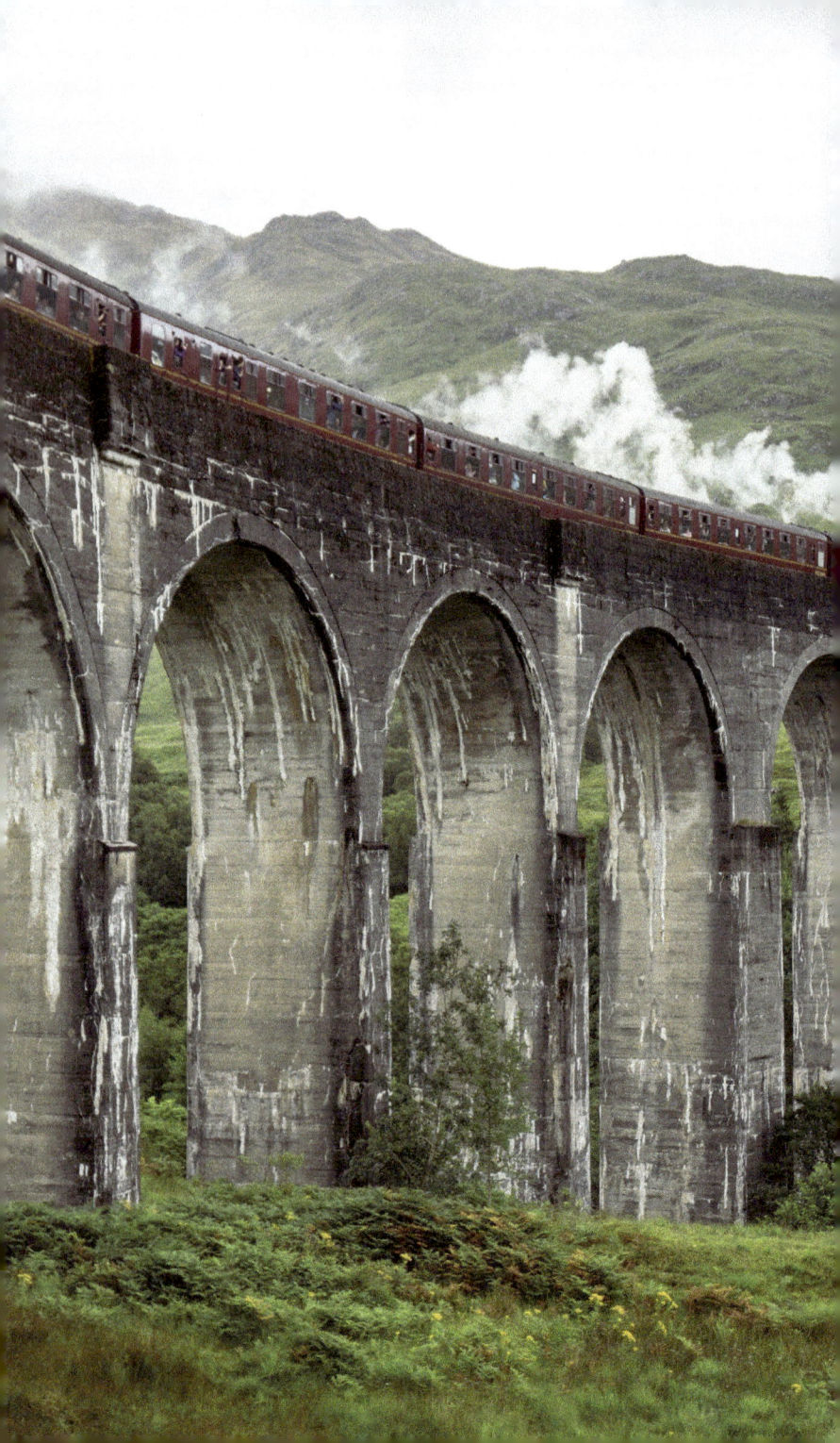

CPSIA information can be obtained
at www.ICGtesting.com
Printed in the USA
BVHW020458120719
553192BV00027B/301/P

9 780464 029168